MOON HUNTER

"Sweet Becca, I am sorry."

Mack bent and gently kissed the scar on her shoulder, sending a shiver down her back.

She was torn between pleasure and fear. She should be afraid of him, of his touch, but part of her craved it more deeply than she had ever wanted anything. "Why are you sorry? It was none of your doing?"

"I am sorry for all the pain you've suffered. You deserve something much better from life." He brushed her hair away from her neck with the back of his hand and traced a path along her shoulder with his lips. The soft, satiny pressure of his mouth should have tickled, but instead it caused a tremble in her legs.

Something stirred inside Becca, and she felt herself weakening. She should move away, run away. She should not let him touch her so, but it felt . . . She could not even put words to the sensations he roused with in her. Suddenly she was not sure that she could run away, that she even wanted to.

She wanted his touch.

She wanted him.

MOON HUNTER

DEANNA MASCLE

Zebra Books
Kensington Publishing Corp.

http://www.zebrabooks.com

ZEBRA BOOKS are published by

Kensington Publishing Corp.
850 Third Avenue
New York, NY 10022

First Printing: June, 2000
10 9 8 7 6 5 4 3 2 1

Printed in the United States of America

To
My grandparents who believed I could do anything,
My parents who taught me I could be anything,
My husband who loves me despite everything.

CHAPTER 1

The thin wail of a baby's cry drifted through the moonlit clearing.

The hair rose on the back of Mack's neck, even though he knew it was only a screech owl. He tightened his grip on the cool metal of his long rifle and scanned the forest around him.

Tiny rustles in the dried leaves under the trees revealed the movements of night animals, but nothing bigger than a possum stirred within his eyeshot. The moon was so bright he could see quite a distance.

Despite his near certainty that he was alone in this part of the Kentucky frontier, he tugged his black felt hat down to a more secure position. Mack knew the moonlight would glint off his silvery blond hair as easily as sunlight did, and he didn't want to attract any unwanted attention. He liked his hair right where it was—securely attached to his scalp.

The owl's cry did not disturb the night again, although he could hear the cooing of a mother raccoon and her babies on the other side of the clearing. After waiting a few more heartbeats, Mack moved on. Despite the size of his tall, muscular body, his moccasins made no more sound than the raccoons did. He stepped through the pine needles and dead leaves lining the animal track he had been following for the last hours on foot, after leaving his horse hidden in a ravine several miles back.

No one could possibly know he was traveling through this part of the territory, but still Mack stopped regularly to cock his head and listen to the night sounds around him. He knew there were war parties making their way through Kentucky. That was why he was here—to warn the settlers who had built their cabins apart from the bigger stations and forts.

He could well understand their desire to make their own way. Silas "Mack" McGee was well known for his intolerance for the rules and boundaries of civilization. He just wished more of the folk who chose to live in these places were better able to protect themselves and didn't bring their women and children with them. The helpless had no place on the dangerous Kentucky frontier as many settlers learned to their peril. Too many times his warning missions ended up being a burial party because he arrived too late to do any good.

Although the killing of Captain James Estill and much of his militia troop, by a Wyandot war party near Little Mount in March, had stirred many homesteaders to move to the bigger settlements, there were still those determined to stay in their homes—no matter the cost. And it had cost a number of them their lives in the months since the British pushed the Indians back on the warpath.

But not this time, he hoped. He had one last stop before he hightailed it back to the fort. He had reached everyone else in time, and with luck he would be in time for this family, too. He had heard this settler's wife had a baby. That could very well be why he was hearing phantom babies cry in the night.

It was bad enough burying the adults who had chosen to take their chances on the dangerous frontier, but touching the small corpses of their children brought back bitter memories and only strengthened his own resolve.

He would never marry.

He would never have children.

Loving a woman, making children with her, was just too risky, even for Mack—a man who lived for risk. He had inherited his father's blue eyes and ability to charm the ladies, but unlike his father, Mack reserved his flirtations for the type of woman who didn't want a commitment. He knew when to be cautious.

It was this caution, and his ability to move so quietly, that kept him alive during these turbulent times in Kentucky. That and luck. Mack was a big believer in luck. He had seen far better woodsmen than he lose their scalps to nothing more than ill luck.

Only a lucky man, or a crazy one, would volunteer to scout the area around Fort Boonesborough for Indian sign, and yet that was how Mack made his living. Maybe it was his way of repaying an old debt. He tried not to think about it too often. Whatever the reason, it was his duty, and Mack always fulfilled his duty. It was all he had—all he was.

The owl cried again. Closer this time. The sound echoed eerily, as if the owl was nesting in a hollow tree, and Mack's skin prickled. While he knew a screech owl's cry could sound like a human baby, this particular owl sounded too human for his comfort.

The moon slid behind a cloud, and dark eased over the forest. Still moving forward, Mack concentrated on the noises around him, waiting for the next sound, trying to pinpoint the location of the owl— or whatever creature wailed in the night.

His foot came down on a rock, knocking him off balance, and Mack stumbled to his knees. Anticipating an attack when he was at his most vulnerable, he rolled to the side and came up still clutching his rifle. Turning his head to quickly scan his surroundings for any sign of danger, Mack looked directly into a pair of frightened green eyes that stared at him from a white face framed by a tangle of red-gold curls.

"Fancy meeting you here." The stranger sounded more amused than surprised, and he flashed her a quick grin before turning away from her to quickly scan their surroundings. Apparently satisfied there was no immediate danger, he knelt down beside the broad base of the hollow tree that sheltered Becca and her baby. "Didn't mean to drop in on you like that."

It was a measly shelter and truly provided no protection from beast, or man, but she couldn't stop herself from shrinking back as far as she could go and raising the hunting knife she had stolen from her husband before running out into the night. "Don't touch me."

"I won't." He settled back on his heels and looked her over, his full mouth curving into a frown.

She eyed him warily. Clad in buckskins and moccasins, he looked more woodsman than settler. Most of the men she knew wore homespun and boots. Yet with his blond hair and blue eyes he was no Indian. He might be a renegade—although she doubted it. She didn't think a renegade would keep his distance just because she asked it.

There was something about the handsome stranger that made her want to smooth the tangles from her hair and return his smile. He seemed gentle enough, his voice was low and smooth, and he hadn't touched her. But Becca had learned the hard way not to trust men—no matter how handsome, no matter how nice they seemed. Hugh had been nice to her, a long time ago.

Never taking her eyes off him, Becca shifted the baby so that she shielded Caroline with her body. "Who are you? What are you doing here?"

"I'm Silas McGee, most recently of Boonesborough, but you can call me Mack. I'm just out making social calls. I've come to pay my respects, ma'am." After respectfully tugging at the brim of his hat, he gave another quick glance around. "You wouldn't have a cabin stashed around here somewhere, would you?"

"Why do you want to know?"

The smile he gave her was obviously intended to be reassuring, but life had drummed into Becca long ago that the things that made a man smile often boded ill for their women.

"I need to talk to your husband."

A shiver of fear shook her, and she clutched Caroline so tightly the baby whimpered in protest. He was a friend of Hugh's. When she had escaped the cabin that evening, while Hugh rummaged in the root cellar for a jug of corn whiskey, she had hoped to escape the worst of his temper. Tomorrow, after he had slept off his binge, he would be more reasonable, and if he beat her, it would only be a token punishment, not the result of a violent rage fueled by liquor.

But if this friend had come to help him in his search, she didn't have a chance. She couldn't hope to elude two grown men in the forest at night—not with a baby—and she wasn't going to leave her child behind.

"Keep following the trail. The cabin's over the rise and a bit." The effort it took to hold the knife at the ready was making her arm tremble, but Becca wasn't about to put it down. She would not give up without a fight. She wasn't big enough to fight off Hugh—drunk or sober—and she doubted she would last more than a minute with this large stranger; but that didn't mean she would make it easy for him. She would not go willingly.

"I'd be happy to escort you home, ma'am. I'm sure the night air can't be good for the baby." He reached toward her.

Becca hissed a warning at him, and he froze.

She knew he was right. The night air wasn't good for the baby, but she suspected the air inside the cabin wasn't good for the baby either. "We're staying here."

The stranger narrowed his eyes at her. "Is everything all right, ma'am? Has your husband seen Indian sign about?"

Becca bit back a humorless laugh. "There's worse things than Indians, mister. You go on down to the cabin and see for yourself. Then you can see what a fine figure of a man your friend Hugh Wallace makes. You're big enough to hit back, so he probably won't take a lick at you."

"You're hiding from your husband?" Silas McGee frowned at her. "Come with me. I'll make sure he doesn't hurt you tonight."

"And what of tomorrow and the day after? I own, there's nothing you can do to help me." Becca didn't try to disguise her bitterness. She didn't let it rule her, she wouldn't let her bitterness sour Caroline's life, but she would use it to give her strength to endure—and to find a better way for her daughter. Her mother had done nothing to protect her. Becca would do better for Caroline.

Mack studied Becca for a long minute. "You'll fight me if I try to bring you with me."

It wasn't a question, but she answered him just the same. She wanted no misunderstandings. "Yes."

His mouth twitched into a smile. "You realize it wouldn't take me but a minute to drag you out of there."

So like a man, finding humor in her weakness. She tightened her grip on the knife, preparing for his attack. "I know, but I'd make you pay the price in blood. You might not think it worth the trouble."

"I think you are right." He stood up and tipped his hat to her. "Good night, Mrs. Wallace."

In the blink of an eye he disappeared from her view. She couldn't even hear the rustling of his steps, but then she hadn't heard his approach, though she had been straining her ears in case Hugh came in search of her. What white man could move so silently through the woods? The way Hugh stomped and cussed he could be heard for miles, but this Silas McGee was silent within an arm's length.

Maybe he hadn't left at all.

The idea of the stranger lurking just outside her sight sent a chill down Becca's spine. Perhaps she should make a run for the cabin after all. There were worse things than a beating.

If the stranger was indeed a renegade, he could mean to take Becca and Caroline captive and sell them to the Indians or British—or he could mean to simply kill them here. She refused to think about the stories of rape and torture she had heard.

She forced herself to take a deep breath. She was being ridiculous. He was no renegade. He was probably long gone and didn't want anything more to do with a crazy woman who slept in trees. She refused to acknowledge the faint trace of regret she felt at his leaving. If there was one lesson she had learned during her short, brutal life, it was that no man was worth her regret.

The silence outside the tree was deafening. Unable to stand it any longer, Becca leaned out just enough to scan the clearing and saw him.

The stranger was sitting on the ground with his back against a nearby oak tree. His long rifle lay cradled across his arms, and his hat was tilted low over his face; but she could still see the gleam of his eyes in the moonlight.

"Did you need something, ma'am?" He asked in that low, quiet voice so unlike her husband's rough bellow.

This man was different from her husband in so many ways, but she knew that didn't really mean anything. Hugh had been different from her stepfather at first, but when it came down to it, he had treated her the same.

"I need you to be gone." Fear and anger warred within her, but she allowed only the anger to show in her voice. A year of marriage to Hugh Wallace had taught her not to reveal her fear.

"I'm sorry, ma'am, but I can't oblige." He didn't raise his voice, nor did he did sound angry; but Becca had no doubt he meant to stay.

That spurred her anger. "Why not? You were on your way to see my husband, so just keep on going." *And please, God, don't bring Hugh back here.*

"Can't do that." He spoke in the same firm voice.

Glaring at him, she noticed for all his apparent stillness that he was on the alert. His eyes constantly surveyed their surroundings, and his long-fingered hands were never far from his rifle. She began to wonder if he was really a friend of Hugh's.

Despite her best efforts, she felt her fear slowly overtake her anger. "Who are you, Silas McGee, and what are you doing here?" she asked softly.

"The name is Mack. Whenever someone calls me Silas I look around for my father."

He grimaced so quickly, she wondered if she had imagined the haunted look on his face.

"Mack, what brings you out here in the middle of the night? This is hardly the time for social calls."

"My duty."

That was no answer, and the hardness in his tone accentuated her fear. She put her hand on the knife. It wasn't much protection, but it was all she had. "What is your duty?"

He shrugged. "I do what has to be done, what others are afraid to do, this and that."

Becca narrowed her eyes at him, tightening her grip on the knife handle. She didn't like things she didn't understand, and Silas McGee was a mystery. "So which is it right now?"

He turned and met her eyes. "Tonight I'm looking out for you."

Unable to read his expression, and unwilling to let him see the fear in her eyes, she looked away. "Why?"

"Why? Because you can't, Mrs. Wallace."

CHAPTER 2

Something screamed in the night.

Becca woke with a start. Her heart pounded as she realized she had fallen asleep, protected only by a hollow tree and a man she didn't know. Then she remembered the sound that awakened her, and her breath caught in her throat.

There were even worse things to worry about.

Something screamed again.

Trying not to panic, she struggled to sit up and identify the sound. Her sudden movement jolted the baby into wakefulness, and Caroline squawked in protest.

The stranger, Mack, was beside them in an instant. He touched Becca's shoulder with a gentle pressure. She could barely make out his form in the partial darkness that was slowly lightening in the east. "Can you keep that baby quiet?"

"Yes." She matched his low whisper. "What was that? A catamount?"

She felt more than saw the quick shake of his head. "Could be a panther, I reckon, but ..." He shrugged. "I'll go see. You keep the baby quiet in case it ain't."

"She's just hungry." Becca answered as she eased the baby to her breast, modestly half turning away from the opening of the tree, but by the time she had fumbled the buttons of her bodice free, he had already disappeared into the darkness of the forest.

Another horrifying scream rent the air, and Becca bent her head to press her lips to the gentle curve of Caroline's head. The stranger was right. It wasn't a catamount. She didn't want to think about what it had to be.

The woods around her were still in the predawn light. No birds called. No animals moved in search of food or a sleeping place for the day. Everything was quiet.

A light breeze rattled through the leaves, bringing with it the scent of wood smoke and the stench of burned meat. Pressing her back against the tree in an instinctive gesture to hide, Becca shivered at the implications of those smells and held her baby tightly.

A clatter of rifle shots shattered the still air and echoed through the forest. Becca flinched, nearly pulling her nipple from Caroline's mouth. The screams halted, but she could hear more chilling cries and whoops from the direction of her cabin.

What if something happened to Mack? What would become of Becca and Caroline then? Her survival had somehow become intrinsically linked to this man she didn't know and didn't trust.

As if sensing her mother's distress, Caroline squirmed in her arms. Becca soothed the baby with a gentle caress, drawing comfort from the living warmth of her child, and began to pray.

She had never been one for much churchgoing— she had never lived near enough to attend one regularly—but her mother had taught her to read from the Bible, and she had memorized many of her mother's favorite psalms to soothe her during the months when she lay dying. They had never brought much comfort to Becca before, but just now she needed to believe in something that had the power to protect her and Caroline.

"Even when I walk through the dark valley of death, I will not be afraid, for you are close beside me, guarding, guiding all the way."

She recited the rest of the Twenty-third Psalm and continued with the Lord's Prayer until she sensed a presence at her side. Suddenly remembering the knife she had let fall to the ground while she slept, Becca fumbled in the dirt for it as she turned to face the intruder.

Gripping it so tightly it hurt her fingers, she positioned the knife between her baby and the opening of the tree trunk. She lowered the knife when she saw it was Mack standing before her.

His eyes flickered to the knife, and he flashed a quick grin. "Prayer can't hurt—we sure can use all the help we can get—but I'm a firm believer in the Lord helps those who help themselves. Now get out of that tree; we're moving out of here fast unless you'd rather go with that Shawnee war party that just killed your husband and burned your cabin.''

"Hugh's dead?'' She bit her lip so hard she tasted blood. She had known it must have been Hugh screaming, but it just didn't seem real. Only yesterday he was the biggest threat to her life and Caroline's— and today he was dead. She hadn't loved her husband. He had done everything to ensure she hated him; but they had made a child together, and she could still feel sorry for what could have been. "You're sure?''

"He looked dead enough to me, although he was alive when they put him in the fire. When they started shooting their rifles I took a chance and made sure. They didn't hear my shot." Mack gave her a level look. "There was nothing else I could do. I couldn't save him. Even if I'd managed to get him away from the war party of at least ten braves, he wouldn't have lived. They'd already cut him pretty bad. They waited to burn him until they were already sure he was a goner. I would have tried to save him if I could, but I couldn't take that risk. Risking myself means risking you and the child. Right now, *you* are my first consideration.''

"I'm sure you did everything you could," she said softly, touching Caroline's cheek gently. She didn't believe him, even though he had stayed to watch over her this night—a fact that surely had cost Hugh his life. In her experience men said many things to make themselves look important.

As for the fact he had guarded her last night, she

was sure he had his reasons. She couldn't imagine what they were, but there had to be some benefit in it for him. That was the only reason a man ever did anything—to benefit himself.

Taking a moment to refasten her bodice, Becca handed him the baby and crawled out of the hollow tree. Then she pulled out a small bag that now contained her worldly possessions. Everything else had surely been destroyed in the cabin fire. It didn't matter, not really. All she cared about was Caroline, and her baby was safe—for now. Slinging the bag over her shoulder, she reached for her child and noticed her hands were trembling.

Mack studied her with narrowed eyes. "She's a little mite but still a lot for you to carry for any distance; can you do it?"

"I'll have to, won't I?"

Mack had never met a woman quite like this one, though he had learned a long time ago that Kentucky made a special kind of woman. He had watched Rebecca Boone follow her husband into the Kentucky wilderness at the cost of her two children—her oldest son tortured by an Indian she had once welcomed into her home and her youngest son stillborn after the grief and worry of their loss. He had watched women tend their injured menfolk, hack homes out of the wilderness and pick up rifles to protect their families from attacking Indians.

But he had never seen a woman carry her child in her arms through the wilderness, knowing full well the savages that killed her husband could be following behind, and yet never once look back.

She was a tiny little thing; the top of her head barely reached his shoulder. And despite the fact she was curved in all the right places, she didn't seem to have an ounce to spare anywhere. This morning she was so pale her green eyes fairly glowed in her face, but she never once faltered in spite of her obvious growing exhaustion.

She kept moving, fueled only by the handful of dried corn he had given her to eat on the move and her own fierce determination.

He had offered to carry the baby for her—once. She had refused in no uncertain terms.

"You need your hands free to protect us," she said flatly. "I'm not much of a hand with a rifle, and I doubt you can shoot while holding a three-month-old baby. I'll take care of Caroline, and you take care of the rest."

It warred with every chivalrous instinct, but he knew she was right. There was no room for chivalry on the frontier—more proof, if he needed it, that women did not belong here. But that did not matter at the moment; belong or not, she was here, and he was responsible for getting her to safety.

And they weren't moving fast enough.

There was no time to cover their trail, not that it would do any good if the Shawnee were searching for sign, but he would feel more comfortable if their back trail was not so clearly marked. He had counted on putting in more distance from the cabin, but then he wasn't used to traveling with a woman.

He didn't plan to do it long enough to get used to it either, not wanting the responsibility of a woman and child, but now that they *were* his responsibility, he would do his duty by them. He hoped it wouldn't be the death of them all. Determination would not be enough to see the woman to safety. His skill would help, but it would come down to luck—and she looked like she was plumb out of that commodity.

Casting a sidelong look at her, he saw she was slowing again. She caught his eye and squared her drooping shoulders. He couldn't help but admire her spirit and determination, but knew neither would be enough to see her through the danger around them. The baby mewled in her arms.

He tightened his jaw. They didn't stand a chance, but Mack was determined to give them one. "Keep the child quiet. That sound carries too far in the woods."

Fury flashed in her eyes despite her exhaustion. "She cannot help it that she is hungry and wet, and I do not believe the sound carries all that far."

He narrowed his eyes, grabbing her upper arm to wheel her around to face him. "You do not believe? How experienced are you on your own in the woods to know such a thing?"

"Experienced enough." She angled her jaw. "We were managing just fine before you stumbled upon us, and we will manage just fine after you leave us." She curved her lips into a smile as if she had scored a point.

"I stumbled yes, but I heard that child's cry long before I did so. I imagine the war party that killed your husband heard it, too, or they will figure it out when they sober up."

That made her eyes widen and her mouth tighten. "I didn't know," she said softly.

"Of course you didn't. There is a lot you don't know, but if you stick close to me and do as I say, *exactly* as I say, I might be able to get us out of this alive."

Fear kept her on his heels as the sun crept higher in the sky; but as the morning progressed, she flagged more and more behind him, and the baby refused to be quieted by her soft pleadings.

He turned a glare at them. Her skin was nearly translucent with exhaustion, but rage lighted her eyes as she cradled her child against her shoulder. "I cannot keep her quiet any longer. She is wet and hungry. The only way to quiet her now is to stop and tend her needs."

When he took a step toward her, she clutched the child to her chest as if afraid he would take the baby from her.

"Keep her quiet." Lifting his head, he scrutinized the area to gauge their location. "We can stop up ahead."

"She's—"

"We'll stop up ahead." He took another step toward her, intending to prod her forward, but her instinctive flinch halted the gesture. The idea of a woman fearing him set his teeth on edge, but he didn't soften his expression or his tone. "Keep moving and find a way to keep the babe quiet."

He turned away from the anger in her eyes and

led her down the trail to Boonesborough and safety, where he could be shed of this responsibility. Anger was better than fear, but he would use both if he must, so long as she did what he told her. He did not mean to earn her affection—only see her to safety.

Moving as quickly as he dared, Mack did not need to turn to know she followed. She had quieted the baby, but not silenced it entirely. It would have to do, for he knew he had pushed her as much as he could.

She kept pace with him for a time, but gradually slowed as her exhaustion overcame her strength of will. Still, she did not complain, and she didn't stop walking until he held up his hand to signal a halt. When he turned to face her, she swayed slightly, like a sapling in the wind. He put out a hand to steady her. The fact that she let him touch her was not a good sign.

The only sounds in the still air were her ragged breathing and the muted chatter of water over stones. She lifted her head and took a faltering step toward the water, but he grabbed her arm in a rough grip. "Wait."

"But please . . ."

"I said wait."

"You're enjoying this, aren't you? Making me beg, ordering me about just to suit your whim," she snarled at him, futilely trying to tug her arm free.

He loosed her so quickly she nearly fell.

This time when she stumbled and he reached for her, she shook him off. When she made no move toward the water, he let her be. If she wanted to waste her alloted rest time arguing with him, then it would be on her head.

"No, ma'am, I'm not enjoying this at all. Looking out for you is certainly not suited to my whim, and there is nothing to enjoy about risking my neck for a woman."

"You don't like women."

It was not a question, but he answered it anyway. "I like women just fine. I just don't believe women have any place on the frontier and certainly not out in some lonely cabin, but I will see you to safety."

"Why?"

Her question made no sense to him. She might as well ask the bird why it flew. "Why what?"

"Why are you doing this?" She shifted the baby, grimacing at the weight in her arms. "You've made it clear as day you want nothing to do with me, so why help me?"

"It is my duty."

"Why risk your neck for it? Is duty that important to you?"

"It is everything."

She gave him a long look. "And how have I become your duty?"

"I was sent to warn you of danger. I didn't arrive in time, so now you're my duty until I've seen you to safety."

"I don't see how driving me to exhaustion and starving my child can serve your duty. If we die before we reach safety, then you've failed."

"Yes, but if we stop every time that child cries, we will be scalped before sunset."

She tightened her hold on her child until the baby squirmed in protest. "Then, do it." The words were no more than a whisper of defeat.

"Do what?" He would have no misunderstanding.

"Your duty, just do it. I will do as you say so long as I understand where your duty lies."

He shook his head. "You do not need to understand. You only need to do as I say."

Her eyes narrowed. "I am not bound by duty. I will do as I wish."

And that wish would see her dead, but he could not, would not, let that happen.

"Do you want to live? Do you want your child to live? Then, I suggest you listen to me, Mrs. Wallace, because there will be times when I give you an order, and if you obey, then you have a chance to live, but if you do not, then most likely you will die—and your child with you. Is that what you want?"

"You know it is not."

"Then, we understand each other. Now drink and tend your child. We move on as soon as you've done that. But first let me see there is no trouble along the riverbanks."

He stepped to the edge of the trees and scanned the shoreline for any sign of watching eyes. The water was peaceful with no sign of movement but a lark, swooping in to catch water bugs hovering above the still pools at the river's edge.

When he waved her foward, she made her way to the fast-running creek, avoiding his eyes as she walked past him and carefully lay the baby in a bed of leaves. When Mack came to stand beside her as she drank, she gave him a dark look. "I'll be quick. I don't want to slow you down."

"I won't leave you behind, Mrs. Wallace."

"Of course not, your duty again."

"As you say, Mrs. Wallace."

She flashed him an unreadable look. "You might as well call me by my first name. Under these circumstances it seems rather silly to be so formal. I'm Rebecca, but my family's always called me Becca."

"Well then, Becca, I promise I won't leave you behind."

The small, thin hand that stroked her child's back trembled slightly. Mack could read her fear in the tense lines of her body and the tiny lines of worry between her eyes.

"I told you that I won't leave you, and that includes the child. No matter if she's screaming her head off and it brings down a whole tribe of Indians upon our heads. I give you my word."

"And what is that worth?" She blazed at him, her eyes filled with fire and her hand reaching in the pocket of her skirt for the knife he knew she had hidden there. "What will such a promise cost me?"

From a man, those words might have stirred his anger, but Mack already knew she had little reason to trust in any man. "Everything. Nothing."

"What is that supposed to mean?"

"Those are the answers to your questions," he said quietly. "When I give my word I mean it, so that promise means everything, and the promise will cost you nothing."

"Why should I believe you?" she snapped at him.

He closed his eyes. Remembered again the small, still figure of his dead sister lying in the snow stained crimson by her blood. Remembered his mother's corpse reaching out with one hand, even as she cradled his baby brother to her with the other, reaching for the help, the mercy, that wasn't there.

He opened his eyes. That was enough to remember. He would do his duty this time, even as he had failed it before. "Believe me because I do this not for you, not for me, but to repay a debt I owe."

CHAPTER 3

She believed him.

He was protecting her to pay an old debt. There was no need to ask why she was the recipient of his aid. Somehow she knew the woman he wished to help was long dead. She just wondered what that woman had been to him. And then she wondered why she cared. At least now she could better understand his devotion to duty—and why she benefited from it. It was strange to think she could depend on a man. She doubted she would ever trust him, but she believed him when he said he would see her safe.

Becca saw pain and loss in the deep blue depths of his eyes before he turned away to once again study the shadows along the riverbank. The idea of his suffering disconcerted her. She wasn't used to thinking about a man's feelings. In the past, all she had cared about was judging a man's mood to predict when the next violence would erupt.

In fact, until this moment she had not really been sure that men even *had* feelings. Or at least the finer feelings. She knew they wanted things. Just thinking about the things men wanted made her shiver.

Mack gave her a quick look. "Are you cold?"

Another surprise. She had never met a man so concerned with her well-being. Until now, men had only cared about her if it affected them. Was she well enough to make dinner? Would she lie still while he—

She pressed her lips together tightly and stopped that thought. Hugh was dead. It was not right to think ill of the dead. She cast a quick look at the stranger who had rescued her from sure death. He was her protector, but that didn't mean she had to like him or let him know her every thought. In her experience, it was better that men didn't know what you were thinking. "I'm fine."

"Then, let us move on as soon as you've seen to the child. Tomorrow you can ride, if you like. My horse isn't far from here."

"Ride or walk, I'll do what I have to." Becca shrugged as she gathered her child up with aching arms and tried not to think about walking another step. She had survived all the brutality her life had thrown at her this far; she was not about to let a simple thing like being tired stop her now.

"But what do you want?"

"What do I want?" she echoed, unsure what he meant. Her husband and stepfather had never asked what she wanted. They had just told her what they wanted. It made no never mind to them what she thought.

"We'll make better time with you mounted, but if you're afeared of riding, you needn't."

"I'm not afraid," she said, still marveling over the fact he had asked her opinion. He was a hard man, but there was softness in him, as much as any man could have. "Thank you for asking. That was very kind."

His face hardened as if he was embarrassed she would notice his kindness. "Some women are foolish about such things."

"Riding horseback or thanking men for their kindness?"

He narrowed his eyes. "I am not a kind man. Do not mistake me for one, and we will deal well with each other."

She lifted her chin. "I am not a foolish woman. Do not mistake me for one."

"I will not make that mistake again." He grinned at her.

The sudden appearance of his smile made her catch her breath. The glimpse he had allowed her of his inner torment had touched her heart, but his smile—well, there wasn't any use in thinking about that. She was done with men for good now that Hugh was dead. Now that she was free to make her own way in the world, it wouldn't be with a man.

Caroline rooted at her dress, making small grumbling noises.

"I'm going to nurse the baby now." Becca told

him quietly, sorry to disturb the easy condition they had just discovered.

"You'd best. I don't think they followed us, but we're not out of danger yet. We need to get moving on as soon as you've finished."

He shifted his body so he was facing away from her, but he did not move from his seat on a rock only a few feet from Becca and the baby.

She raised her hand to the buttons that fastened her bodice and hesitated as she gave him another quick look. Realizing he didn't mean to move farther away, she loosened her bodice enough to allow the baby access to her breast and adjusted Caroline so she could nurse. The baby greedily attached herself to the nipple.

Becca must have made a small sound of surprise because Mack suddenly turned on them, swinging his rifle up even as he moved. Giving their surroundings a quick scan, he relaxed back down on the rock.

"I'm sorry," he said softly. "I would give you more privacy, but it's just not safe."

She caught her lip between her teeth as she studied him, searching for the familiar signs of revulsion that so often led to a beating. What she saw on his face puzzled her.

There was no revulsion, no quickening anger. Instead, his expression gradually softened until he looked almost wistful, as if the sight of her nursing her child brought back a warm memory. Then his face hardened once more, and she knew his memories were no longer pleasant.

Always on the alert for any sudden masculine

change of mood, Becca's blood began to race. She fixed her gaze on his hands so she could brace herself for the expected blow.

"Please . . . just let her finish. Then I will put her down." She curved her body around the baby, preparing for the expected blow. Often, Hugh hadn't waited until she put the baby down before he started beating Becca.

When several heartbeats had passed and no blow fell, she looked up and saw Mack staring at her in open astonishment. "Your husband beat you for nursing his child?"

"If I did it where he could see and hear. He said it was disgusting, that she was like a leech sucking the lifeblood out of me." As her fear slowly drained away, Becca straightened again. She kept forgetting that this man was very different from her dead husband. "You do not find this disgusting?"

"No. It is beautiful. You are beautiful."

When he turned away, she realized it was not disgust that he wanted to hide from her, but something private that he was struggling to master. Silas McGee was a very strange man.

They walked the morning away and much of the afternoon. When Mack finally signaled her it was time to stop, Becca sank to the ground in exhaustion. She barely registered the fact there was a sheer cliff face behind her and the sun had all but disappeared behind it.

Her body was strong from days filled with hard work—sometimes Hugh even pressed her into helping him in the fields—but nothing had prepared her for walking for hours while carrying her child.

Fine-boned like her mother, Caroline was not a big baby nor a chubby one, but her weight had pulled on Becca's arms and shoulders until she lost all feeling in them. Becca had feared she might lose her grip entirely and drop the baby, but she had kept Caroline safe by sheer force of will—for now.

When Mack lifted Caroline from her arms, Becca stirred with a cry of distress, fumbling in her skirt pocket for her knife.

"It's all right," he said soothingly to Becca as he tickled the baby's cheek with his lips.

Caroline crowed with delight and tried to catch at his mouth with her tiny fist. She wasn't tired at all, having slept soundly while rocked by the motion of her mother's steps. Soon she would be hungry again.

Seeing her daughter so happy in this man's arms made Becca's heart twist strangely in her chest. No one else had ever held her baby and made her laugh. Caroline had never reached for anyone but her mother.

Then his smile faded as his mouth twisted and his eyes shadowed. He held Caroline toward her. "Take the child. I have a lot of work to do before dark falls."

Becca grimaced as she struggled to her feet and raised leaden arms to take her daughter. Just accepting the light weight of the baby pulled agonizingly on her muscles, but she gritted her teeth against the pain.

Something stomped and thrashed behind the

clump of bushes near the base of the cliff, startling Becca so she stepped behind Mack for protection.

Whatever beast was in there didn't seem to worry Mack a bit. He laughed as he leaned his rifle against a tree and spoke to the hidden creature. "You just relax a minute more and I'll have you out of there."

When he started pulling bushes away from the cliff face, Becca realized the greenery screened the opening to a cave. Mack made quick work of his makeshift wall and soon revealed the ugliest piebald gelding she had ever seen.

A spot of white encircled his left eye, making it look enormous, while a splotch of tan was centered almost perfectly between his eyes, giving him the appearance of a cyclops. His body was covered with patches of black and white that seemed to run together in places to create a muddy gray. And on top of that, the horse was huge. She would never be able to climb on it by herself.

In addition to his sorry appearance, the horse stomped and snorted causing Becca to keep her distance from the apparently disturbed beast. Mack expected her to ride this monster tomorrow? She wasn't sure if it would be better than walking. She would rather die of exhaustion than be thrown and trampled by this creature.

Mack must have seen the doubt on her face. "Don't mind Joseph, he's just in a hurry to take care of business. He doesn't like standing in his own filth and is just letting me know it."

"Joseph?" She had never heard such a ridiculous name for a horse.

"Can you think of a more fitting name?" Mack asked with a grin as he untethered the horse and led him from his small enclosure. "You must admit his coat is many colors."

Smacking Joseph on the rump, Mack sent the horse trotting off into the trees in the general direction of the stream they had passed on their way to the hidden cave.

"That it is." Many colors. That was a kind description of the horse's unusual coat. She couldn't help being curious about the horse, though. "Most men wouldn't want anything to do with such an ugly beast."

Mack laid a finger to her lips. "Quiet. He might hear you. He thinks he is very handsome, and I hate to break his heart by telling him the truth."

Turning her head, ostensibly to search for the horse they were discussing, but more to move away from his hand, Becca was disturbed by the tiny flip-flop in her stomach that started at his touch. "Shouldn't you be looking after your horse?"

"Joseph can take care of himself. He'll come back soon enough." Mack shrugged and moved into the mouth of the cave. He came out toting a pair of saddlebags which he left at Becca's feet. "I'll go collect some wood so we can start a small fire. I've got some cornmeal in one of those bags. You can mix up some corn dodgers for supper. Maybe I'll get lucky while I'm looking for firewood and catch a squirrel off guard so we can have something to go with them."

Still puzzling over the man and his strange relationship with his horse, Becca sorted through the contents of the saddlebags. She sensed a presence at her back a moment before soft lips touched her nape. Turning in a confusion of panic and some emotion she couldn't hope to identify, she found herself nose to nose with the horse. Without thinking, she smacked Joseph on the nose for scaring her half to death and looked up to see Mack laughing at her over an armful of wood.

"What's so funny?"

"You should have seen the look on your face. It's your own fault, anyway. In Joseph's eyes, or rather nose, you are irresistible."

"Irresistible?" She planted her hands on her hips and narrowed her eyes at him. She didn't like being made fun of. Especially by a horse.

"You smell of roses, Becca, and there's nothing Joseph loves more than to nibble on sweet, tender rosebuds. I can't tell you how many times I've had to pick thorns out of that horse's tongue, and that's no laughing matter."

She couldn't help herself. Even though she still didn't like him laughing at her, she couldn't help smiling at the mental picture he had drawn of picking thorns out of his horse's tongue.

"You have a beautiful smile, Becca. You should use it more often." All trace of laughter was gone from Mack's voice as he stepped closer to her.

She recognized the look in his eyes and was suddenly glad his arms were full of wood. He wanted her. She had learned to fear that look in her husband's eye, but in less than a day of knowing Mack, she felt herself drawn to him.

The hunger in his eyes frightened her, but not as much as the unfamiliar response it stirred in her. She couldn't identify the emotion, more of a sensation really; but it made her stomach feel queer, and she didn't like it one bit.

She picked up Caroline, who had been lying nearby in a nest of Mack's clothes pulled from the saddlebags. Hugging the baby to her, she took a step back from him.

The light in his eyes died out, and he dumped the load of wood at the edge of the clearing. He laid the limp bodies of two dead squirrels beside the wood. She had been so preoccupied, she hadn't noticed he had carried them, too. "You better get the fire going. I'm putting it out as soon as the daylight fades. It's too easy to spot the flames at night."

He turned and walked away without looking back.

She tightened her grip on the baby until Caroline whimpered in protest. Kissing her daughter on the cheek, Becca laid the baby back in her nest and knelt to start building the fire. Her hands shook as she carefully built a small pile of twigs and brush, and it took her several tries with the flint to strike a spark.

Then she picked up the still whimpering baby and put Caroline to her breast. "He is coming back. Don't worry, baby, he's coming back."

"Fool!" With a flick of his wrist, Mack sent another stone skipping across the stream. Or rather, he had meant to send it skipping. Instead, it sunk, like . . . well, a stone. "Imbecile."

He knelt beside a deep pool and picked up the water skin he had laid by the stream's edge. After filling the skin with water, he picked up his rifle again. He had had no right to look at her like that. No matter that she wasn't the first pretty widow he had ever flirted with, but he had never forced his attentions on a woman who had been widowed that very day.

And he had forced his attentions on her. He hadn't laid a finger on her, but she had felt threatened. By him. That didn't sit well with Mack at all. He was supposed to protect her, not scare her.

He knew how little she trusted men—and with good reason. She had made it perfectly clear she only tolerated his presence for his protection. He doubted she would even put up with that if it wasn't for the baby.

And he had frightened her. He had seen the panic in those wide green eyes. Not that she had backed down. No. Not Rebecca Wallace. She had glared at him, sending the unspoken message that she would fight him with every fiber of her being. She was feisty, for sure. That had to be what drew him to her.

There was no other good reason for his interest in Rebecca Wallace. Sure, she was a pretty little thing with her red curls and sweetly curved body, but he had known women who were prettier—and willing. Becca was anything but willing. She had damned little softness in her, and all of that was reserved for her daughter. Of course, he had always liked his women strong and feisty. Soft women didn't last long on the Kentucky frontier.

And no woman lasted long alone. He had already left her alone too long. Taking long strides on the path back to their camp, Mack was suddenly struck by the stillness of the afternoon.

No birds called. No small animals moved about the forest as twilight drew near. The hair on the back of his neck seemed to stand on end, and he stepped up the pace while making every effort to move even more silently. Then he heard the baby scream.

"Damn you to hell, Silas McGee, for your carelessness." He slammed his free hand against his thigh as he started to run. He had never let a woman distract him from his duty before. He only hoped Becca and Caroline wouldn't pay for his mistake, that they already hadn't.

Caution checked his haste. Stopping near the edge of the clearing, Mack positioned himself behind a boulder and carefully leaned in for a look.

A large warrior held Becca, twisting her arms behind her back. Although she was obviously in pain, that torture was not what forced her face into a study of agony. The source of her anguish was the warrior's companion who held Caroline upside down, swinging the baby by her heels over the open fire. Caroline screamed again.

CHAPTER 4

Time slowed down until she felt each beat of her heart reverberate through her body. There was a terrible rushing noise in her ears that made her child's cries sound far away. Becca and her baby would be dead in a matter of seconds if she didn't do something.

"Don't hurt my baby!" Panic overwhelmed her as she fought to pull free of the Indian's grip, but he held her firmly. The rancid smell of the slick bear grease smeared on his chest made her gag. Her ineffective fighting seemed to amuse him, but she couldn't stop—not when there was still a chance to save her daughter. He laughed at her as he tugged at a red curl that escaped her braid during her struggle.

Turning at the laughter, the man dangling Caroline above the fire called out something in a language she didn't understand. The baby whimpered in his hands. A mad surge of rage swept over Becca as she redoubled her efforts to fight free. Before the Indian holding her could answer his partner, someone responded from the trees in the same guttural language.

She didn't know what was said, but it was obvious the two Indians in the clearing didn't like it. Her captor shoved her so her skirt skimmed the flames, and she nearly landed in the small fire at the other Indian's feet. The second Indian sneered and tossed Caroline at her. She caught her baby to her breast as Caroline screamed in outrage at the rough treatment.

Although Caroline was no longer in imminent danger, there was no time to comfort the baby as a rifle roared from the trees. The Indian standing closest to her went down with a hoarse cry. His warm blood splattered Becca and Caroline as he hit the ground beside them, still gripping the rifle he had never had the chance to fire.

Becca stared at the body, watching the man's hands twitch on the gun stock, and then his eyes went glassy as he died. Suddenly realizing she could not protect Caroline in this mayhem, Becca tucked the baby behind a nearby boulder where she would at least be safe from stray bullets.

Worrying about the other Indian, she looked up as Mack raced across the clearing toward them, wielding his still smoking weapon above his head. The remaining Indian smiled grimly as he raised his rifle, and Becca realized the man would shoot Mack before her protector could stop him.

Glancing quickly around her, Becca seized the cast-iron pan she had laid on the fire in preparation for making corn dodgers for their supper. The heat of the handle seared through her skin, and she let go before she could put her full weight behind the blow. However, the pan had enough momentum now to knock the Indian in the back of his legs just as he fired. Mack cried out and fell to the ground.

Ignoring the fallen man, the Indian turned on Becca with a roar of pain. Throwing his rifle aside, he drew a tomahawk from his belt and raised his arm.

Becca scuttled back, her heels digging into the soft dirt as she tried to push herself away from her attacker. Bumping into the body of the dead Indian, her free hand touched the cool metal of his rifle. There wasn't time to put the gun to her shoulder and brace it. She barely raised it when the Indian closed the space between them. He cocked his arm back, ready to deliver a crushing blow. Closing her eyes, she pulled the trigger on the rifle.

The kick of the weapon threw her shoulders against the boulder where she had hidden Caroline, sending a shooting pain down her back and knocking the breath out of her. She lay gasping for air, afraid to hope, but when no blow came, she said a quick prayer and opened her eyes.

The Indian lay on his back, his face a gory mess. She had to turn away as bile burned the back of her throat. Reaching behind the boulder, she clutched her baby to her, tighter than Caroline approved, but Becca couldn't seem to loosen her grip as she took comfort from her daughter's screams of protest. Looking up, she fixed her gaze on Mack. He at least seemed to be all in one piece, even though she was sure he had been shot.

Mack managed to stand with the help of his rifle as a crutch. He grinned at her. "Well, Becca Wallace, you're a good woman to have around when things get lively. That was a clever move with the rifle. I've never seen its like."

"Neither have I," she admitted and grinned back at him as relief swept over her. She was alive. Caroline was unhurt. Mack was. . . .

"You're hurt!" The trail of blood oozing from a wound in his calf stained the sandy soil a deep red where he had been standing.

Becca stood on shaking legs and moved to help him closer to the fire. She pushed him down, more than a little frightened at how easy it was. Beads of sweat dotted his forehead, and tension tightened his jaw as his grin faded.

He must be in a lot of pain.

"You rest here. I'll see to the wound and then brew you some willow bark tea. I saw some willow trees not too far back. That should help the pain." She knew she was talking too much, but she couldn't think about anything except the fact that Mack was hurt.

"It's not too bad." Despite his reassuring words, his breath hissed out, and he grimaced as she touched his leg, seeking the wound.

It was impossible to see how badly he was hurt with all the blood. "I'm going to have to cut the leg off your buckskins so I can take care of this." Becca bit her lip as she studied his leg, trying to judge the best angle to start cutting.

Mack gripped her elbow when she reached for her knife. "Never mind that. Just bind it up for now."

Becca rubbed her forehead, grimacing at the trail of sticky blood she left on her face. "I have to treat it. Binding it probably won't stop the bleeding for long. You can't lose so much blood without fainting or—"

"Just do it. We don't have time for an argument, woman!" he snapped at her.

"If we don't take the time, you won't have any time left at all!" she shouted back at him, fear and anger overwhelming her innate caution. She had never shouted at a man. It felt good.

He glared at her for a moment, obviously struggling to find the right words. She knew enough about Silas McGee to know he wasn't accustomed to explaining himself. "If you bind it up tight, I'll do. You take care of the things that need to be done. It's not safe to stay here."

Sensing the urgency behind his words, she bit back her own angry retort and instead asked softly, "What do we need to do?"

"Bind my wound and I'll tell you."

The next hours were a blur for Becca as she put aside her own fear and exhaustion to do what had to be done. Her body ached, and yet she started at each nighttime sound from the forest around them. It was only the sound of Mack's patient voice, talking her through each task, that kept her focused.

She bound up his leg to slow the flow of blood from the wound on his calf. As Mack delivered careful instructions, she reloaded his rifle and the weapons of the two Indians they had killed, laying them beside the wounded man. Somehow she managed to drag the two dead men into the hidden cave and cover the opening with branches. Then she packed up the saddlebags with the few belongings they had used to set up camp and saddled Joseph when he responded to Mack's whistle.

When all was done and nothing remained of their struggle but the bloodstained earth, the wounded man, and her weariness, Becca helped Mack to his feet. She gritted her teeth as he leaned heavily on her shoulder, swaying despite the steadying arm she had put around his waist.

She didn't have to glance back at the ground where he had sat to see how much blood he had lost. She hoped this spring where he intended them to hide was not too far. She doubted he could stay conscious for long. She didn't want to think about what would happen to them if Mack lost consciousness. She wouldn't think about what would happen to them if Mack didn't wake up.

When Mack finally sat in the saddle, sagging and swaying in a frightening manner, Becca leaned against the horse's neck and thanked Joseph tearfully. She had never seen a horse stand so steadily and patiently. She apologized to him for thinking him ugly and hitting him on the nose.

Then she bent to pick up her daughter and followed the horse into the darkness.

* * *

When Mack woke he was surrounded by green. Sunlight filtered through pine boughs that made a makeshift lean-to overhead. He was lying on a bed of blankets covering still more pine boughs.

Not sure where he was, he didn't move and only opened his eyelids a small slit while he tried to remember.

The nearby whimper of a baby brought back a rush of memories, and he jerked his head around to look for Becca and Caroline.

The sudden movement caused an explosion of pain in his head. Tensing his body during the onslaught started a nagging ache in his calf. He gritted his teeth and fought back the moan of pain that nearly escaped him.

Small, cool hands touched his forehead, pushing him back against the pine boughs, and then moved to straighten the blanket that covered him and check the bandage on his leg. He didn't need to open his eyes to know who touched him. Becca always carried the scent of roses on her. He would know her in the dark of night just by her scent.

"Quiet now, I know it hurts, just drink some of this and you will feel better." She held a tin cup to his lips, and he obediently swallowed the bitter mixture until she took the cup away.

Then she moved behind him, resting his head in her lap, and began rubbing his temples. The scent of roses enveloped him, and as the pain in his head began to ease, he slipped into sleep.

It was night when he woke again. Becca lay curled alongside him, her feet tucked neatly against his legs for warmth. The moon rode high in the sky as full and round as a lemon drop above them. He turned his head, slowly, remembering the pain he had brought on himself before, to look at Becca.

She was asleep. Her red curls gleamed in the moonlight against the creamy skin of her smooth cheek. One small fist lay curled around the long rifle she cradled against her.

He frowned at that. It was his responsibility to protect her, and he had failed. She had killed a man because he couldn't protect her. He could not let her down again.

The nagging ache in his leg reminded him that he had already let her down twice. This last day or so he hadn't been able to protect her.

A movement drew his gaze from Becca's face to the small bundle nestled between him and Becca. Caroline stared up with wide eyes that blinked owlishly at him. Her tiny rosebud mouth opened in a perfect "O" as she yawned and then tried to cram her whole fist into her mouth. She gummed her hand while watching him solemnly.

He stroked the baby's petal-soft cheek and smiled at her. "Hungry, are you? So am I, but we can let your mama sleep just a little while longer, can't we? She's awful tired I think."

Turning his attention back to Becca, Mack knew he had told the baby the truth. There were deep circles of exhaustion under her eyes, and her skin was so pale it was nearly translucent. She was even snoring just a little, the sound so soft it was more like a purr, but it brought a smile to his lips. Then he remembered the reason for her exhaustion, and he frowned again as he tried to rise.

Waking with a start, Becca leaned up on one elbow and touched his forehead. "Are you in pain again? Are you feverish?"

"I will do. You are the one who needs taking care of." He spoke more roughly than he intended, angry with his own weakness.

Before he could apologize for his brusqueness, Becca slipped from beneath the blanket and moved to collect the tin cup she had laid nearby. When she brought it to his lips, he pushed it away.

"No."

A tiny pucker of worry appeared between her eyes as she studied him. "You need to take something for the pain."

"I need to be alert so you can rest. I'm not taking that stuff when it knocks me out."

He saw a brief flash of anger in her eyes before she pressed her lips together and sighed deeply.

"Do you know how sick you are?" she asked quietly.

"I am well enough." He managed to lean up on one elbow. He hoped there was no visible sign of the spinning in his head caused by that slight movement.

"Are you?" She raised one eyebrow as she studied him, her lips twitching slightly. "Do you remember how we got here?"

"I brought us here. I remember leading us to this spring very well," he lied through gritted teeth. It had to be the truth. This spring was well hidden, and though Mack had used it often enough on his scouting and hunting expeditions, he had never seen sign of another human using it. The only way they could have made their way here was if Mack had led them.

"You remember nothing because you were dead to the world by the time we arrived here." She shook her head at the memory. "I thought you were *dead* because there was so much blood soaking the leg of your buckskins and I could not rouse you. When you fell from Joseph's back, your wound started bleeding afresh, and I knew then you were still alive, if barely so. Dead men don't bleed."

"I am not bleeding now and neither am I dead."

"It was a near thing, and you are in no condition to push yourself further. You need to sleep. You need to heal." She bit her lip. "Have you thought about what will happen to me and Caroline if you die because you are too foolish to take care of yourself?"

She was right, but he hated to admit it. In the end it was the worry in her eyes that made him give in. He took the cup, hating the weakness that made his hand tremble as he drank her potion, and allowed her hand to steady his.

He lay back down again, exhausted by the effort of arguing with her, but he had to know one thing before he slept. "How did we get here if I did not lead us?"

Becca smiled and nodded her head at the horse grazing on the other side of the spring. "Joseph brought us here. I've quite come around to your way of thinking. He is a wonderful, handsome beast."

Mack fell asleep with the sound of her laughter in his ears.

Caroline's cries woke him. The sun was dipping low in the sky, and he was as hungry and irritable as the baby lying beside him. He had the patience not to show his ill temper, but his patience was strengthened by the knowledge that Becca would not let her baby cry long.

He was right. Caroline had just reached a roar of full rage when her mother scooped her up with one hand while setting a steaming mug beside his hand.

"Drink that up. Just be careful, it's quite hot. I imagine you need it by now." She settled on the ground, turning away from him as she unfastened her bodice to let the baby nurse.

Mack could see nothing but the fall of Becca's hair, but he could tell the moment Caroline achieved her goal. Silence reigned over the small clearing. He sighed with relief. Although his head did not throb like it had the day before, too much of that level of noise would surely bring back the headache with a vengeance.

"How come you're not drinking?" she asked him without turning around.

How could she know?

"You said to let it cool." He didn't have any intention of drinking another of her potions. He was restless and didn't want to go back to sleep so soon. He still felt weak and his leg ached, but nothing he could not master on his own.

"It is not that hot. I promise your body needs this more than you think."

"What I need is some food." There was an edge to his voice, put there by the delicious scent of something cooking on the fire. It smelled like meat of some kind. And all he got was more damned tea. How did she expect a man to heal on such weak fare?

"What did you have in mind?"

"Whatever you've got roasting over that fire would be just fine," he said politely.

"Drink up what's in that mug, and if you can keep that down, we'll see about going to solid food."

"I'll be damned if I'll drink what's in this mug without getting some food in me."

"You're already damned, Silas McGee, and what's in that mug is all you're getting," she snapped at him. Becca didn't turn to glare at him, but he could see the line of tension in her straight back. "I tried giving you solid food last night, and you couldn't keep it down. Drink that broth and be glad of it."

Broth? He leaned closer to the mug and sniffed. The delicious aroma he had detected had been coming from this source and not the fire. He picked up the mug carefully, his hands trembling slightly, but he didn't spill a drop as he sipped.

After taking in the mug's contents, Mack's hunger was abated, and even the pain in his head seemed to ease.

He sighed in contentment, setting the empty mug aside. "How is it you know so much about healing? You are little more than a child."

"My mother taught me." The warmth that had filled her voice only moments before was gone. Not even the anger he had stirred existed any longer. Now her tone was flat and emotionless.

"She must have been a wise woman to have taught you so well."

"She taught me out of necessity. When my stepfather beat her, she wasn't always able to make the poultice or draught she needed to heal herself. By the time I was six or so, I didn't even need her to watch over my shoulder during the preparations."

Mack closed his eyes against the knowledge of her wretched life. He had known how terrible her marriage was, but he had hoped her earlier life had been happier. Obviously this was not the case.

Some women would have given up long ago, but not Rebecca Wallace. She still had the courage to fight for her life, to protect her child, to care for him. He could not understand where her strength came from and how she could still find an ounce of tenderness within herself.

Although her tale was sad, Mack was curious to learn more about Becca. "Is that why your pain medicine also causes the patient to sleep?"

"It was the only way my mother could escape." She spoke softly and kissed her baby's head as she laid the sleeping child beside him on the bedding and picked up the cup he had emptied. "Toward the end, she preferred to know nothing of this world at all."

Becca moved to the fire to refill the cup.

"I can understand why." Mack settled Caroline's limp form so he could better reach her. He loved to watch her sleep, her small, warm body pressed against his hip, her rosebud mouth closed around her pinkie finger.

"I cannot." Becca knelt beside him. Her delicate mouth pressed into a tight frown as she scowled at him. She hadn't buttoned her bodice all the way, and he caught a glimmer of white skin and the hint of the valley between her breasts as she leaned over him. "As long as I live I will never give up. As long as I live I will fight to protect my daughter. I will not let *my* daughter suffer while I sleep."

She thrust the cup at him with such a sudden motion, some drops slopped onto her hand. She licked them off absently as he took the mug from her and set it down on the ground again.

"Neither will I sleep when you and your daughter need me. Lie down and rest, Becca. I will watch over you."

"Drink this first and then I'll consider your offer."

He shook his head. "If I drink this, then I will not be able to stay awake, and well you know it."

Her lips twitched into a smile. " 'Tis only more broth, you of the suspicious mind. I thought you said you were hungry."

"I am hungry, but I need something more substantial than this to take the edge off my hunger." His gaze fell to the opening in her bodice as he spoke. "You promised me more if I drank the first cup."

Becca saw the direction of his gaze and blushed as she hurriedly fastened the remaining buttons. Her smile disappeared, and the frightened look returned to her eyes, only to be quickly replaced by one of anger. "My advice is to enjoy the broth, Mr. McGee, because that is the only thing of substance you will be receiving from me.''

She moved to pick Caroline up, but Mack caught her hand before she could lift the baby. She tried to pull herself free, but despite his weak state, Mack was still stronger than she.

He cursed himself for frightening her yet again. Would he never learn to guard himself around her? The problem was that he had never had to guard his tongue, or actions, around a woman before. He had always chosen the object of his flirtations carefully so there would be no danger of expectation.

Rebecca Wallace did not fit the usual type of woman he chose, and yet he was cursed with this unwitting attraction to her. He vowed he would restrain himself in the future. It would only be a few more days, and then he could safely deliver her to Boonesborough. Surely he could control himself until then?

''Do not fear me, Becca. I would never hurt you and I would never force you.'' Having given her his promise, he released her hand.

She pulled away from him as if she had been burned. ''I know you believe you are a man of your word, but I have learned that a man's word is as fleeting as the wind. Do not bother to make me promises you cannot keep.''

CHAPTER 5

"You are a mystery, Becca Wallace," Mack whispered to the sleeping woman beside him.

She turned at the sound of his voice, but did not wake. He gently traced the line of her jaw with his fingers. Her lips curved into a soft smile beneath his touch.

"Who are you?" he whispered into the silence as he struggled to understand her.

On the one hand, she still did not trust him. He often caught her watching him out of the corner of her eye, and when she was not tending to his needs, she sat well out of his reach.

However, when he did need her, she was there beside him with food or water or anything else he might require. He knew she was helping him because she needed him to guide her to safety, but it was not her need that made her hands gentle on him when she changed his bandages. It was not her need that made her shave him when he complained about the scratchy beard he was too weak to hold his hand steady to shave.

She did not trust him when she was awake, but sleeping was another matter altogether. He smiled as he brushed one red-gold curl back from her face. When she slept she lay beside him for convenience and safety—or so she had taken great care to explain when he finally convinced her to lie down for a brief rest.

When she first lay down beside him, her body stiff and ramrod straight, she took pains to make sure there was plenty of space between them. However, when exhaustion took over and she fell asleep, the truth came out.

In her sleep, Becca gradually moved closer to him, cuddling against his warmth. When Mack touched the sleeping beauty at his side, she did not move away; she did not cry out in fright. None of these things happened. Instead, she smiled and sighed.

She might have great reason to distrust and fear men, but there was something between them that made Becca less wary, less guarded, when she was around Mack. With each hour that passed, he could sense her softening toward him.

And if Becca herself was a puzzle, then his reaction to her was even more of one.

Smoothing her hair back from her face, he decided he could watch her sleep for hours. He had never

known there was such contentment in watching a
woman sleep. Mack was a great admirer of the fairer
sex. He enjoyed their company and sharing their
beds, but he had never simply spent time with a
woman before.

Although he knew some women as friends, namely
the wives of his male friends, he had never suspected
he could find such peace with a woman. Always
before, they had fallen into two categories. Women
in the first category belonged to someone else or
were seeking a husband and were therefore off-limits
to Mack. Women in the second category were content
to share their time and beds with him without wanting
anything permanent.

Rebecca did not fit into either category. She was a
riddle he could not solve, but he wanted her nonethe-
less.

There could be no doubt about that. The scent
of roses that always seemed to accompany her was
beginning to stir a craving in him stronger than it
ever had in his horse.

Lying so close to Becca's plump, inviting lips without claiming them was more temptation than any man
should have to bear. Even with her dress buttoned to
her neck, he could imagine the creamy white breasts
concealed beneath the blue linen. Each breath she
took pushed those breasts against her bodice and
made him long to free them from their bondage. He
might be weak and ill, but he was still a man. He
suspected Becca was enough woman to tempt even
a dead man.

Dead or alive, he could not give in to that temptation. He frightened her. She did not trust him. Given time, something they did not have, he might overcome both, but he knew he wouldn't try, couldn't try. A woman like Becca meant a home and a family. A commitment he was not capable of giving.

But a man could still dream, Mack thought, as he skimmed his hand across the silk of her hair. And he could touch, while she slept trustingly at his side. Murmuring in her sleep, she turned into his caress, rubbing her cheek against his hand like a cat.

Her face tilted up to him, her lips slightly parted. It was all Mack could do to resist the temptation to claim those lips with his, to slide his tongue into her mouth and tease her awake. He lay back with a groan of frustration.

"Mack?" She was awake in an instant, leaning over him, touching his forehead. "Do you have a fever?"

"Yes," he admitted through gritted teeth, but when she would have risen to brew more of her bitter tea, he stopped her with a hand on her arm. "No, 'tis nothing. Go back to sleep."

She shook her head. "It is almost time to feed Caroline again, and you need your rest. You are far from well and should not push yourself so hard too soon. You go to sleep. I'll keep watch."

He was tired, but not really sleepy. He could tell he was on the mend and not nearly as weak as she seemed to think. However, at Becca's insistence he lay back and tried to rest. He was glad he had done as she said, because it seemed her trust in him extended to when he was asleep as well. When the baby awoke demanding to be fed, Becca did not move from their bed of pine boughs. Instead, she opened her bodice without turning her back to him and lifted Caroline to her breast.

Becca's pale skin gleamed in the moonlight, the round curve of her breasts achingly beautiful. He had never dreamed the sight of a mother nursing her child could be so sensual. He had told her before the act was beautiful, and meant it, but now it stirred something in him that was deeper and darker than the gentle admiration of something beautiful and good.

When Caroline fell asleep again with a tiny sigh of contentment, Mack nearly cried out a protest. He wished the moment could go on forever. However, when Becca refastened her bodice he, too, nearly sighed, in relief rather than contentment.

Fully clothed, Becca Wallace was a temptation, but with her breasts bared to the worshipping light of the moon, she was captivating—and Mack had vowed he would not allow himself to be captive to any woman.

"Lie still and rest." Becca gritted her teeth and shoved Mack back onto his blanket. She kept her hand firmly in place against his chest to make sure he stayed there. The last time she put him back to bed, he got up again as soon as she turned her back.

The morning had been a constant battle of the wills between them.

So far she was winning, but just barely.

When he lay still for more than a heartbeat, she lifted her hand, and he promptly raised himself up on his elbows.

She glared at him. "Stay."

Knitting his eyebrows together, he frowned back. "I am done resting. Let me alone, woman."

"Let you alone?" She rocked back on her heels and folded her arms across her chest. "What would have happened if I let you alone when that Indian was going to shoot you dead? What would have happened if I let you alone after you were shot? What would have happened if I let you alone while you were feverish? What then?"

After giving him something to think about, she stood up and deliberately turned her back on him, busying herself with cleaning up from their morning meal. She did not turn and look at him. From the gentle, rustling sounds behind her, she did not think he was lying still. But neither did it sound like he had tried to stand up. There would be no gentle rustling then, she knew, simply a loud thump as he hit the ground.

Finally she heard the sound she had been hoping for, a sigh of resignation. "You win, woman. I will stay put, but if I lose my mind from the boredom, it will be on your head."

She turned and gave him a quick smile of approval. "You may lose your mind, but I promise you will not lose that leg if you mind me."

He scowled at her. "I said I will stay put; I never agreed to mind you."

She ignored that. He had agreed to stay put, and that was all she wanted from him. "If boredom is your only concern, then you can watch Caroline for me while I check my snares." She set the baby beside him, her heart twisting to see how Caroline smiled up at him.

He let the baby pull the tip of his thumb into her mouth and gum it, but his attention was on Becca now. "Snares?"

She knelt to feed more wood to their small fire. She didn't want it to go out while she was gone. If she caught anything in one of her traps, she would have to cook it before night fell and she put the fire out. There might not be enough time for that if she had to start a fresh fire. "How do you think I caught that rabbit?"

"I thought you might have shot him; after all, I've seen evidence that you're a crack shot."

She shrugged to hide her pleasure at his compliment. "I'm a fair shot, but I didn't know if it was safe to hunt so close to the spring. I didn't want someone to hear the shot and perhaps discover us. A snare seemed more certain, and I did not need to leave you for long."

"I told you before, Rebecca Wallace, and I find it more and more true every day, you are a wise woman." He gave her an approving smile.

"Then, you would be a wise man to listen to me." She left the clearing before she let herself smile in answer.

She was still smiling even after she checked all her snares and had collected one fat turkey for her trouble. She had caught a rabbit in another snare, but some varmint had already been at it during the night. She threw the remains of the rabbit into the brush and reset her trap. The loss of the rabbit did not trouble her. The turkey would provide more than enough meat for the two of them.

She would roast her catch in the coals of the fire, and tonight Mack could have his first solid food since his illness. Since she did not have to hurry back to check on him and the baby, Becca decided to collect some greens to go with the turkey. She was plenty tired of corn dodgers and squirrel. Tonight's meal would be a tasty change.

As she searched out greens, Becca hummed softly to herself and even stopped to pick a wildflower and tuck the bloom behind her ear. The action stopped her short as she had a sudden realization.

She was happy.

She was a widow of less than a week. She and her baby were dependent on a man still weak from a bullet wound and fever, a man she knew little about. They were alone in the wilderness where any war party or marauding wild animal could attack them. She had no home for her daughter and no certainty of what the future would bring.

And she was happy.

Becca shook her head in disbelief. More than once Hugh had told her there was something wrong with her head. This just proved it. She had nothing to be happy about, except maybe the fact her husband was dead, and even that was truly not something to celebrate. So why was she happy?

Mack's face filled her mind. Those deep blue eyes that watched her so intently. The sensual mouth that widened into a slow grin. The silver-blond hair that glinted in the sunlight.

She shivered and rubbed her arms as she realized what was happening. A widow of less than a week and already she was weakening. She had vowed that if she survived Hugh, she would never allow another man to have control over her.

Silas McGee was not Hugh Wallace. Their short acquaintance had already taught her that, but that did not make him a better risk. Hugh had been different than her stepfather. Hugh could be apologetic and tender, when he was sober, and then beat her savagely when he was drunk. Her stepfather was brutal and cruel—drunk or sober. Mack did not seem to be like either one of those men, but that only made her worry more. What kind of man was he?

She sank onto a flat boulder, setting the turkey and greens beside her. She lay back and took in a deep breath, trying to sort through her conflicting emotions. The scent of pine filled the air from the tree standing beside the boulder and only added to her confusion. After sleeping beside Mack on a bed of pine boughs for days, she thought she might forever associate the tangy scent with the man.

What made her crave him so much that the simple

scent of pine needles brought his face before her mind's eye? Nothing she had seen in her mother's marriage or her own had led her to believe there was ever anything tender between a man and woman. Every touch she had ever received from a man had caused pain—until Mack.

Though he had never caressed her, never done more than offer her support or steady her over rough trail, somehow she seemed to know his touch would be gentle. And she yearned for it.

She wanted to know the feel of his chiseled lips on hers. She wanted to know the touch of that lean, hard body against hers. She wanted to know the sensation of being loved by a man.

The only problem was that Becca did not believe in love, at least not between a man and a woman. She loved her daughter, believed strongly in the bond between mother and child, but knew nothing between a man and woman could withstand a man's brutal nature. Her mother had believed in love, and ultimately that belief had killed her. Becca would not make that same mistake.

For her sake and for Caroline's, she *could* not make that mistake.

Her conflict resolved, Becca gathered her food and made her way back to the camp. She found Mack and her daughter asleep. A soiled linen lay nearby in a crumpled pile.

He sat, leaning against his saddle, Caroline's head tucked under his chin. One tiny pink fist clutched his hair even as the baby slept. His strong arms cradled her daughter gently against his chest, just as Becca wished he would hold her.

She tightened her jaw. Kindness to her child would not win her over that easily. She would not think about the fact her stepfather had never given her a kind word or gentle gesture in all the time she lived under his roof. She would not think about the fact Hugh had never held his daughter so tenderly or changed a dirty linen.

She could not afford to think about those things. For all the ways that Mack was different from the other men she had known before, he was still a man.

Becca cleaned the linen and then moved to claim her daughter.

"Leave her. I'm afraid if you move her she will wake up, and I had the devil's own time getting her to fall asleep." Mack rubbed his eyes with his free hand.

Becca laughed as she lifted the child and settled her on a blanket nearby. "Nothing wakes her once she is asleep except an empty belly. I expect that will come soon, but we are safe enough for the moment."

Mack eyed the sleeping child as if expecting her to explode into wakefulness. When she did not, he leaned back with a sigh.

"Thank you for tending her." Mindful of her renewed vow, Becca did not look up at him and immediately set to plucking the turkey and preparing it for roasting in the coals. She did not need to look at him. She could well remember the way his tanned chest lay half exposed beneath his unlaced shirt and the way his hair was tousled from sleep.

"Don't thank me. It was the least I could do after leaving you responsible for everything else from tending my wounds to keeping us all fed."

Despite her resolve, Becca felt a flush of pleasure creep across her face. "Still, it is not man's work to care for a baby."

"It is not woman's work to go hunting either, but you did it."

She would not be swayed by kind words, she promised herself. "I did what I must."

"How is it you are so skilled at setting snares? From what I've heard of your husband, he does not sound the sort to have the patience to hunt in that manner let alone teach his wife the skill."

Becca laughed at the idea of Hugh setting a snare. "You have the right of that. I learned from a half-breed Indian boy. He and his mother lived for a time with the trapper who owned a neighboring cabin."

"Your husband did not mind you spending time with a half-breed?"

Becca shuddered slightly at the memory of the beating those lessons had cost her, but she had considered them well worth the price. Anything that would help her achieve independence was worth the cost. She could not explain all that to Mack, though. "He minded."

After burying the turkey in the coals of the fire, Becca moved to check Mack's wound. Kneeling at his side, she refused to look at his face, concentrating on his leg instead. The wound looked to be healing well, so she quickly washed it and bound it up with a fresh bandage.

Relieved to have finished that task without actually looking at Mack, she picked up the gourd she had used to carry water to wash the wound.

"Becca, hold still so I can talk to you." Mack touched her arm, startling her so she dropped the gourd of bloody water on him.

"Don't touch me!"

She tried to crawl away, but he caught her leg before she could get out of his reach.

She knew he wouldn't hurt her, but she was beginning to learn there were other things to fear from a man's touch. Somehow, someway, she had learned to crave his touch, crave it so much she feared letting him touch her would weaken her resolve.

"Stop, woman!" He spoke forcefully, but it was the gentle regret behind his words that halted her struggle.

As soon as she stopped moving away, he let go of her ankle. "I'm sorry, I shouldn't have touched you."

He was sorry and so was she. She bit her lip, unsure what to say. "I am the one who is sorry, but do not worry, I will have this cleaned up quickly so you can go back to sleep."

When she reached for his blanket, Mack touched her hand to stop her. "Don't. I don't want you to wait on me anymore. I can take care of this. It was only water."

"It was dirty water, and of course I will take care of it. It was my doing."

"It was *my* doing," he said forcefully, retaining his grip on the blanket so she could not pull it away. "I said I will take care of it."

"I want—" She bit her lip, suddenly unsure what it was she wanted.

"I know you want to take care of me, but this time we are going to do what *I* want."

CHAPTER 6

Mack lay back in his bed of pine boughs and suffered.

The pain in his leg had softened from agony to a dull ache. The scent of roasting turkey filled the air, stirring his hunger for his first taste of solid food in days.

His problem did not lie with either his leg or his stomach.

His problem was the woman he could not have.

He wanted her.

Becca hummed as she sat sewing nearby, sunlight glinting off her red-gold curls. She was so beautiful it hurt to look at her. Closing his eyes did not help matters much—not when he had already memorized every nuance of her expression and her every habit.

He knew there was a tiny furrow of concentration between her eyes as she stitched up the buckskins she had cut off him to tend his wound. He knew she would wind a curl of hair around her finger when she paused in her work to watch Caroline sleep.

Finally unable to stand it any longer, he threw back the blanket Becca had laid over him and struggled to sit up.

She was beside him in an instant, outrage written in every stiff line of her body. "What do you think you're doing?"

At least she hadn't touched him. It was bad enough that she was so near it would take no effort at all to pull her into his arms. Frustration added a sharp note to his voice. "Trying to stand; what does it look like?"

"It looks to me like you are a fool. I thought we settled this argument this morning." She scowled at him.

He shrugged. "We did, for the morning. It is now several hours later, and I want to try walking."

"No." She spread the blanket back over him and pushed against his chest in an attempt to make him lie back down.

He resisted her effort and threw the blanket off himself again. "I must. I cannot remain an invalid forever, Becca. We must be on our way, and I must test the limits of my strength now. What if we are attacked?"

Folding her arms across her chest, she angled her chin up and glared at him. "You will be an invalid forever if you open that wound again. If you do not let it heal, you run the risk of infection. Do you want to lose that leg?"

"Better my leg than you or Caroline."

She narrowed her eyes at him. "I don't believe we have to choose between the one or the other. Caroline and I have survived just fine these past few days with you resting that leg so it can heal."

"So far." He let the words hang between them for a moment. "The longer we camp here, the greater the danger."

She gave him a stubborn look, raising her small, pointed chin another notch before answering. "We have remained undiscovered this long."

"How long will we remain undiscovered when we cook over that fire every day?"

"We put the fire out at night so it cannot be seen."

"It cannot be seen, but that is not the only way to find a camp. How far do you think the scent of that roasting turkey carries?"

Her eyes widened, and she quickly checked the positions of the long rifles and her baby. Turning back to him, she narrowed her eyes. "You are trying to frighten me."

He was. "Is it working?"

"Yes, and I do not like it."

He did not like it either. He wanted to hold her and comfort the fear away. He couldn't do that, but he could make sure she was safe. "You must face the truth, Becca. I need to get back on my feet as soon as possible."

"I agree, but this is too soon. Tomorrow maybe."

Her voice was firm, but he could see the uncertainty in her eyes.

He could not afford to be uncertain. He had

learned a long time ago that hesitation on the frontier could cost you your life. "Today."

"You are determined to do this, no matter the cost to yourself?"

"Yes, but I am willing to compromise."

"Compromise?" she asked, giving him a suspicious look.

"Compromise. If you let me up, I will only walk as far as that second pool of water. I will rest and wash myself. After soaking my leg, I will walk back. It is not so far, and I will not do the entire journey all at once. That should not be so bad."

"I do not think you can even make it that far, but it is on your head." She threw her arms up in a gesture of surrender and went back to her sewing, refusing to watch as he struggled to his feet.

It galled him that she was right.

Even with the help of a stout walking stick she had found for him in the woods days ago, so he could at least relieve himself without her help, Mack barely made it halfway to the pool.

Unwilling to admit his weakness and the return of the sharp pain in his leg, he stopped and leaned against the smooth bark of an oak tree to catch his breath and regain his strength. Aware that Becca was watching his every move, he carefully schooled his breathing and refrained from wiping the sweat off his brow.

Only the scent of roses warned him that she was near before she touched his arm. He barely checked the impulse to flinch away from her. He wanted her so much, her very touch burned him. It took all his self-control to stop from pulling her into his arms. Somehow he managed to resist both impulses.

"You cannot make it to the pool. Come. I will help you back to bed." She slipped her arm around his waist.

As he felt her warm curves press against him, Mack struggled for the strength to endure her touch without giving in to his desire. He doubted he could. "Don't help me."

"Stop being such a stiff-necked fool. You need my help."

That was true, but his problem wasn't a stiff neck, and he definitely wasn't going to tell her about it. "Leave me be, woman. I just need to rest for a minute, and then I can make my own way."

He managed a half dozen more steps toward the pool before he could go no farther. Unfortunately there was no tree nearby to brace himself against. Becca stepped up before he could collapse and supported his weight against her slim frame.

"I am too heavy for you," he protested after he managed to catch his breath.

"I am stronger than I look, and you are more foolish than you look."

At least this time she did not try to help him back to bed. Somehow, together, they managed to bring him to the pool's edge.

Mack gritted his teeth as he eased into the water, still wearing his clothes. He had already shown Becca the extent of his physical weakness. He would not subject her to the sight of his lust. He would undress after she left him alone and he was able to use the water to hide the source of his discomfort.

The only good thing about the ache between his legs was that it managed to distract him from his wound. As time went by, the cool running water soothed both. He leaned back against a rock and let the current wash over him.

"Mack, are you all right?"

The worry in Becca's voice jolted him back to reality, and he opened his eyes.

She knelt on the bank, trying to reach for him. Her posture left the bodice of her dress gaping wide, so he could see the breasts that caused him so much torment. Suddenly the water was no longer cold enough to solve his problem.

"I am fine. Can you not let me bathe in peace?"

She looked hurt at his harsh tone, but he was past the point when he could afford to be diplomatic. Maybe she would keep her distance if she was upset with him. He could only hope it would be that easy.

She stood and gave him a cold look. "Call me if you need anything. I brought you some of the soap I found in your saddlebag and a clean shirt."

"Thank you," he replied in equally cold terms. "Now leave me alone."

"Fool. Insufferable pig. Stupid man." Becca paced their now quiet camp, unable to sit and sew as she had before Mack's need to be as stupid as . . . well, a man, had taken over. She checked on Caroline, who was sleeping peacefully, her tiny fists curled beneath her chin and her bare rump pointed to the sky.

Becca put her nervous energy to good use, straightening the camp, feeding the horse and cleaning the greens she had gathered for supper. When time passed without a call from the nearby pool, she started to worry. What if he had fallen asleep and drowned? What if he had tried to make his way back and fallen? He could be lying, helpless and too weak to call to her. He might need her.

Settling her baby on her hip and scooping up a long rifle with her free hand, she rushed to the pool, hesitating just within the shadows of the trees surrounding the water.

For a moment she could see nothing in the pool. Ripples spread across the surface of the water, and she almost threw herself forward to pull his lifeless form to the bank. Then she saw movement beneath the surface and the flicker of white skin.

He was not drowning or dead as she had feared. He was swimming.

She pressed her lips together as she tried to puzzle out how a man so weak he could barely walk could find the energy to swim.

His head broke through the surface, and he flipped his hair back off his face as he gasped for breath. She could see that the effort of swimming had brought him pain and further sapped his strength. His chest heaved as he breathed, his face tight with discomfort. But he was a strong, healthy man, and she knew he was well on the path to recovery.

As he reclined in the shallows, water sluiced off his

tanned chest and drew Becca's gaze lower. Below his waist, his skin was pale in water not deep enough to cover his manhood.

She quickly averted her eyes, flushing in embarrassment despite the fact he could not know she watched.

So he was safe and well. He had not drowned or hurt himself. He seemed well enough to even swim about in the small pool. She had satisfied her mission, and yet she could not move away.

Instead of going back to camp, she turned to watch him again.

He leaned back and tilted his face up to the sun. The lines of pain around his mouth eased as he relaxed and his breathing returned to normal.

Somehow her searching gaze made the transition from assessing her patient's well-being to assessing Mack as a man. She was more than pleased with the results of both evaluations.

He was a handsome man, tall and well-made. His chiseled features and deep blue eyes had surely made many a maiden sigh. More than once when she caught herself watching him, Becca had to stifle the urge to sigh, herself, and she knew better. She knew men were nothing but trouble.

Then, why was she finding it so necessary to remind herself of that fact more and more often? Was she so stupid that she *wanted* to allow another man the right to beat her, touch her, whenever he willed it?

Except Mack would not beat her, and she did want

him to touch her. When she had helped him walk to the pool, when she had put her arm around him, when he had been so close to her she had wanted. . . .

"No."

Caroline squirmed in her arms, awakened by either her mother's soft cry or tensing muscles, and let out a sharp cry.

Becca quickly hushed Caroline and stepped farther back into the trees, but it was too late. Mack was already looking straight at her.

"You might as well come on out, Becca. I know you're there."

He didn't sound angry anymore. Worse. Much worse. He sounded amused.

There was nothing she hated more than to be laughed at. Flushing again, this time in anger, she moved forward. "I was just coming to check on you, to see if you needed any help."

"I'm sure that's exactly what you were doing." He nodded agreeably. "And you just stayed to watch to make sure nothing terrible happened to me."

"Yes," she said, tight-lipped as she tried to avoid looking below his chest. It was a difficult maneuver considering the fact his face was at a sharp angle below her and she had to look down to speak to him. She settled for fixing her gaze on his eyes. "Are you quite done with your bath?"

"That depends," he replied silkily, lacing his fingers behind his head and eyeing Becca beneath heavy lids.

She stiffened. She didn't like the way he was looking at her or the way he was teasing her. "On what?"

"On you." He smiled. "Are you quite done looking?"

The heat of her anger and embarrassment swept the length of her body in a heartbeat. If she hadn't worked so hard to heal him, she might have even considered using the long gun in her hand to finish him off then and there. As if she had any interest in *him* as a man. As if she had any interest in any *man*.

It was time someone set him straight, and she would take great pleasure in doing just that. She spoke slowly, emphasizing each word for effect: "You . . . are . . . a—"

He laughed, cutting her off. "I know. I am a fool, an insufferable pig and a stupid man."

She narrowed her eyes at him, wishing that looks could kill, or at least wound. "You heard."

"It was hard not to. I'm surprised you did not wake the babe earlier."

"I'll leave you to finish your bath. You can make your way back to camp in your own good time. I do not care how long it takes you. In fact, I might prefer it to take all night so I won't have to suffer your company."

Lifting her chin to a defiant angle, she turned on her heel. Before she could take a step, he called out to her.

"Becca, don't go."

She turned back reluctantly, preparing herself for more ammunition to fuel her anger.

He gave her an apologetic smile. "I am sorry for teasing you, but you blush so prettily I cannot resist."

She would not let him off that easy. The compliment did take the edge off her anger, but she wasn't prepared to let him know that. She raised one eyebrow as she stared at him coolly. "At least I can amuse you."

He chuckled. "You do that, Rebecca Wallace, but my mockery is a poor return for all the time you've spent caring for me."

"Yes, it is, but I never expected anything more than ingratitude from a man. It is to be expected."

"I hope you have learned in the time we've known each other that I am not like most men."

Her mouth went dry as he met her gaze and captured it with an intensity that sent another heated flush across her skin.

"You are better than some, but then I've met wild boars more domesticated than my late husband."

"I don't think the kind of man you want is domesticated, sweet Becca."

When he swam to the edge of the pool, Becca took a step back just to keep some distance between them.

"You are right about that," she said softly. "I do not want a domesticated man."

"Then, we may do well together after all. Come join me and scrub my back." He grinned widely.

The brilliance of his smile weakened her; but her bitter past was still stronger, and so she smiled in return.

"I do not think so, Mr. McGee. You see, I want

neither a domesticated man or an undomesticated man."

His smile faded slightly. "Is there another kind?"

"It does not matter, for I want no man, and that includes you."

CHAPTER 7

Becca woke with a start, gasping for breath, her heart pounding.

Fearing an attack, she fumbled for the long rifle on the ground beside her, but as she lay poised to defend herself, she realized the forest around them was silent and empty. There was no threat—unless she counted the man sleeping beside her.

It was only a dream, she assured herself again, trying not to remember his lips touching hers, his fingers tracing her curves. It was only a dream. Only another dream. . . .

For Becca, it was a long night.

When Mack returned from the pool that afternoon, he had made it easy to avoid him, as easy as you could avoid someone dependent on you to care for his wounds. However, he had asked her for nothing and not once engaged her in conversation.

Long after dark fell, she had sat beside the still-warm embers of the fire, debating whether or not to make her bed apart from him after the events of the day. In the end she feared he would need her after his exertions that afternoon, and she had joined him on the bed of pine boughs.

He didn't need her. He slept like a log beside her, not even waking when Caroline had screamed her protest at having her linen changed when she would rather be nursing.

It was Becca who lay sleepless and tense, alert to his every movement.

It was Becca who needed.

Her fingers moved restlessly beneath the blanket. She forced them to her sides—again. More than once she caught herself reaching for Mack.

It was the dreams.

Even now, fully awake, her heart seemed to beat faster than normal, and she could not keep her breathing at an even level. Her skin felt strange—so much more sensitive than usual she could barely stand to lie still beneath the scratchy wool blanket.

She needed.

She could not find sleep. She could not relax. She could not put a name to this need. She was afraid to put a name to this need.

Becca tried to blame her inability to sleep on the nap she and Caroline had shared after leaving Mack at the pool, but she knew in her heart that was not the cause.

It was the dreams. . . .

Finally dawn came, and she rose in an attempt to

put some physical distance between Mack and herself, knowing full well it was too little too late.

He awakened well after sunrise—ravenous and surly—and barely spoke a dozen words to her all morning. Her own temper was prickly from lack of sleep, and the tension in the camp did not improve her mood.

When the sun reached its pinnacle in the sky, she reached the limit of her tolerance. She knew what was bothering him. An active man, he was not accustomed to such long periods of stillness. A fiercely independent man, he never depended on others to take care of him.

She just didn't know what was wrong with her.

She would not think about the hunger in his eyes as he watched her move about the camp. She would try to forget the way he started as if her touch burned him when she checked his wound. She would push the memory of her restless night to the back of her mind. She would not think about the dreams that invaded her fitful sleep.

If only it were that easy.

Sitting on the ground, her back to Mack so she did not have to see his watchful gaze, she wrapped her arms around her legs and rested her chin on her knees. She did not want to think about the dreams plaguing her, but could not help it.

She never dreamed. She could not remember dreaming as a girl, and she certainly never dreamed while married to Hugh. But last night she had dreamed. And what dreams. . . .

Her dreams had been so vivid, so real. She had

dreamed of Mack, of his touch. He had not touched her in all the ways she wanted—no craved—and feared. Instead, his caress had been feather-light, more like the whisper touch of the wind as he skimmed his hand across her hair and traced the curve of her cheek.

In her dream she had not pulled away from him as she did while awake. As she knew she should. In her dream she had reached for him. As she knew she should not.

Even now, hours later, with the sun high in the sky, she did not want to think about her dreams—and their implications. It could lead to nowhere but trouble. Unable to sit still any longer, Becca prowled about the camp, making minute adjustments to the arrangement of their scanty cooking utensils, checking on the baby repeatedly.

Mack growled deep in his chest. "Will you settle down, woman? You are making me dizzy. What is wrong with you?"

It was unbearable.

"Nothing you would understand." Certainly nothing she could explain.

Unable to tolerate the atmosphere another moment, Becca scooped up her daughter and laid the baby beside Mack.

"I'm going to take a bath. Watch her while I'm gone."

Without waiting for his agreement, Becca rummaged in her small bag of belongings for the bar of soap she had packed, then appropriated Mack's spare shirt, which she had washed the day before. She planned to wash her dress and her hair, and she needed something to wear while her dress dried. She left the camp without looking back.

Alone by the spring, she determined she would not think about Mack. Slipping into the cool water of the pool, she could pretend Silas McGee did not exist. She could pretend she knew nothing but bad of men. She could pretend she would never want a man. Except she did want.

"Stop it."

Just saying the words out loud helped stop the path of her thoughts and brought her back to the moment. She had come here to take care of herself for a change, and she would not think about him.

Working up a lather, she scrubbed her dress. After laying it across a bush to dry, she washed her hair. Feeling clean and relaxed, she lay back and floated on the water. Closing her eyes, she half dozed in the warmth of the sun. She listened to the soothing sounds around her: the soft tinkling of the water over the rocks and the buzz of locusts in the distance. Time seemed to stop. She felt as if she were alone in the world. It was a familiar feeling. She had spent many afternoons in the creek near her cabin doing this very thing last summer.

She had been avoiding a man then, too.

Many an afternoon she had run off to hide from Hugh and escape the heat of the day in the water. The prickly heat of summer and her husband's cruel temper had made her pregnancy difficult.

The cool caress of the stream and the solitude had made that summer bearable. She had refreshed her body and laid her plans for her baby. Even before Caroline was born, Becca had been determined her child would have a better future. She had never expected she would have the chance to make those changes so soon. She had never expected Hugh to die.

The cool water lapped against her breasts. The teasing caress reminded her of her dreams and the others change in her life.

Mack.

This time a refreshing bath was not going to make her feel better. He was not going to stay out of her thoughts.

But why?

She caught her bottom lip between her teeth. She did not want anything to do with him. She did not want him. She did not want any man.

How could she be sure?

Her reluctance was based on the type of man she had known before. Her stepfather had made sure she had little contact with any man but him before he arranged her marriage, and Hugh had guarded her even closer after that.

She laughed out loud as she suddenly realized the cause of her problem. It was so simple really.

Mack was the first man she had known who did not hurt her. He was so different from her experience, it was only natural he should fascinate her. She knew now he did not seek to cause her pain, instead offered something other than violence. It was only a short stretch to go from not being afraid of his touch to wondering what it would be like to have a man touch her without causing suffering.

Her feelings for Mack meant nothing. Soon enough they would part, and the fascination would end.

Soon enough.

Satisfied with that perception, Becca rose from the water. The heavy feeling of her breasts told her it was nearly time to feed Caroline again, and she did not like to be away from the baby long. She had spent enough time pampering herself. Maybe she could convince Mack to try walking again, and he would leave her alone. Confident with her newfound knowledge, she did not care if he did not.

After nursing Caroline, Becca settled by the fire so she could watch the squirrel stew bubbling as she brushed her hair dry. The baby lay beside her playing with her toes and gurgling happily.

The warmth of the afternoon and the easing of her tension combined to make her sleepy, but she was not going to risk lying down beside Mack. She felt more comfortable now that she had identified the problem, but that did not mean she wanted to risk being so close to him. It was wiser—and easier—to keep some distance between them. Especially when she was wearing nothing but his spare shirt.

He was a big man and she was a small woman, so the shirt covered her quite respectably. He couldn't see any more of her than showed when she hiked her skirts up to wade across a stream, but she would not feel entirely comfortable until her dress was dry enough to put back on.

If anything, the shirt covered her better because it was not as form-fitting as her dress, but the material was coarser and made her skin feel more sensitive—more vulnerable.

She laid the brush in her lap with a sigh.

"Becca."

Just the sound of her name on his lips made her tense up. But he sounded so strange, she moved to him without stopping to think or even set the brush down. She hoped his fever had not returned. "Are you okay?"

"I'm fine."

He still sounded irritable, but this time when she touched him, laying the back of her hand against his cheek to check for fever, he did not flinch away. She managed to keep her hand steady as well, reminding herself that he needed her. She could not afford to let her little quirks get in the way of his care. She was relieved to discover he was a little warm but his skin was not flushed. She did not think he was feverish.

"How do you feel?"

"Just bored." He shrugged.

"So am I," she admitted, relaxing slightly after she moved her hand away from him. It was easier to maintain her nonchalance when they were not touching.

"I can think of something to pass the time." A smile teased the corners of his mouth.

Becca shifted away. She knew he was only teasing her, but the tension emanating from him told her it would not take much encouragement for that to change.

"I don't think so." She did not fear Mack, but that did not mean she felt comfortable enough to banter with him. The only reason she did not flee was her confidence that she could still outrun him in his weakened condition.

"Relax, Becca." He touched her hand with a quick gesture. "I do not plan to ravish you. I was only going to suggest I brush your hair."

"Brush my hair?" Becca repeated stupidly, not sure she understood. She had been so sure after the way he had been watching her. . . . Was there no end to this man's surprises?

"Brush your hair." He tugged on one damp strand. "I was watching you by the fire and remembering when I was a little boy. I used to brush my mother's hair." His smile took on a wicked edge. "But if you'd like me to do something more, I've had more than my share of compliments in that area as well."

"I do not think your mother would appreciate being mentioned in the same breath as that kind of woman." Becca turned away to hide her flush of embarrassment.

"Becca, they are not the kind of woman you seem to think. They were all ladies, just lonely."

"And I suppose you comforted them." Her voice sounded shrill in her ears. She couldn't think why hearing about his women should bother her. It didn't. She just didn't like to hear about loose women. That was it.

"For a time." He sounded sorry, as if he missed those lonely ladies. Maybe that was not all he missed.

"I don't need your comfort." She stiffened her back beneath the weight of the lie.

"Becca, do not be afraid. I have never forced a woman, and I am not about to start with you." He twined a wet curl around his finger. "I only want to brush your hair. After all I have done for you, how can you refuse me that one favor?"

"After all I have done for you, how can you talk of favors?"

"You have a sharp tongue for a woman who was afraid of her husband." He took the brush from her hand and began to stroke it through her hair.

She had been trying to decide if it would be a mistake to sit so close, but now that he had begun brushing, it seemed harmless enough to let him continue. And he did have a nice touch.

Closing her eyes to better enjoy the sensation, Becca shrugged. "It did not take me long to learn he was going to beat me anyway, whether or not I gave him reason. I decided I would rather give him reason. Sometimes if I could see the mood coming on, I would sass him. He would beat me in punishment, but it would not be as bad a beating as I got when he was in one of his black moods, and then we would be at peace for a time."

"Becca, you are an astonishing woman."

"Why? Because my husband beat me?"

He brushed her hair in silence for a moment before answering, "No, because you did not lose yourself. You kept your strength and your humanity. He beat you, but on your terms. I don't think he ever really dominated you."

"He did," she said softly, more to herself than him. "When Caroline was born he had a new weapon to wield against me."

He stopped brushing for a moment. "Did he hurt her?"

"No, he didn't have to. He'd already learned I could stand a great deal of pain myself—it was harder for him to make me suffer—but then he learned just keeping me from my baby when she cried . . ."

She turned her head so he couldn't see the tears filling her eyes. Even dead, Hugh had the power to torture her. She hated him.

"Don't cry. He's dead." Mack's voice felt like a caress as he leaned closer to her. "He can't hurt you anymore."

"I know," Becca said fiercely, looking down with surprise to find her hands fisted in her lap. "I know he can't. It is wrong of me, but I am glad he's dead."

"Then, we can be wrong together, for I cannot help being glad, too. No man should die the way he did, but the more I learn of Hugh Wallace, I sometimes think he died too easily."

Mack's voice was tight with anger, but his hand remained steady and gentle as he brushed her hair.

It shouldn't have, but his presence comforted her and allowed her to let her anger go. "I don't want to talk about Hugh anymore. I'm trying my best to rearrange my memories of him. Someday I want to be able to tell my daughter about her father without hating him."

"You don't want her to know the truth?"

"The truth is too ugly. I don't want it to taint her

view of the world, of men." Becca wet her dry lips. It was difficult to explain herself. No one had ever cared to hear her thoughts and reasons before. Not even her mother. "And I want her to be able to love Hugh's memory, even if she could never have loved Hugh. I owe him that much."

"You owe him nothing."

She shook her head. "I was his wife. He did nothing to me that was not his due."

"That does not make it right, Becca."

"He had his reasons for being the way he was; some he could not help and some were my fault."

"How could it be your fault? I know you have a sassy tongue, but you said yourself he was going to beat you anyway. How could his cruelty be your fault?"

She bit her lip, not wanting to tell him the truth, but she wanted him to understand. Maybe if he knew the truth he would stop looking at her in that way. "I was a failure as a wife."

Mack laughed out loud. "That was a good one. Tell me another."

She stiffened. "You do not believe me?"

"You've got that right. You are every man's dream, Becca. You are beautiful, gentle, a good mother and a good cook."

"This is not all a man looks for in a wife."

"You do not nag, you do not complain and you can be very good company when you're not as jumpy as a sinner on judgment day. Now you have me curious. Just how were you a failure as a wife?"

"He said I was cold. He said I had no wifely feelings. He said I was a failure as a woman." She closed her eyes, trying to fight back the tears that stung her eyes at the memory of Hugh's anger on their wedding night. "He said if I would not be a wife to him, then he would treat me as a slave."

She could still remember the anguish of his words as they tore into her soul. She had been so hopeful at his initial kindness. But when he tore her nightgown off her and then. . . .

She shuddered at the memory of his rough pawing. She had fought him, scratching and biting when her blows hadn't deterred him, but nothing stopped him from ripping through her maidenhead, then leaving her bleeding and crying to get another jug of corn whiskey. When he went at her again that night, she had screamed in pain and fought him again.

When he was through using her body, he had beaten her and then told her why.

"Becca, forget him. Forget everything he did. Forget everything he said. He is dead and you are not. It's over."

"I can't forget. It's not that easy."

He smoothed her hair and pulled her back against him, cradling her gently in his arms as if she were a child. "You can and you will. You are a strong woman. That is why you survived being married to that monster, and that is why you will go on with your life. You will forget him."

His touch was gentle, but his words were fierce.

She wished they were true. "You don't understand."

"Then, help me understand, Becca. He's not worth one of your tears."

She couldn't find the words to explain. She would show him. Pulling away from him, feeling cold from the loss of his touch, she moved the neck of the shirt to the side so she could shrug one shoulder free.

Twisting her neck, she could see the scar gleaming white in the sunlight.

"Now you can see why I can never forget him. He made sure of that the first week we were married. He branded me. Just like a slave."

Mack traced the letter *H* and then the *W* with a touch so light it sent shivers down her back. "Not like a slave. He didn't use a hot iron to do this."

"He used a knife. He wanted it to be more personal."

CHAPTER 8

"Sweet Becca, I am sorry."

He bent and gently kissed the scar on her shoulder, sending a shiver down her back.

She was torn between pleasure and fear. She should be afraid of him, of his touch, but part of her craved it more deeply than she had ever wanted anything. "Why are you sorry? It was none of your doing."

"I am sorry for all the pain you've suffered. You deserve something much better from life." He brushed her hair away from her neck with the back of his hand and traced a path along her shoulder with his lips. The soft, satiny pressure of his mouth should have tickled, but instead caused a tremble in her legs.

Something stirred inside Becca, and she felt herself weakening. She should move away, run away. She should not let him touch her so, but it felt. . . . She could not even put words to the sensations he roused within her. Suddenly she was not so sure that she could run away, that she even wanted to.

She wanted his touch.

She wanted him.

And yet she could not take the risk. "Mack, stop, please."

Her voice sounded breathless and held none of the forcefulness she had meant to inject. But Mack's lips stilled as soon as the words were out of her mouth.

"You are right. We only agreed to brushing your hair," he whispered against her neck, his breath tickling her skin, sending shimmers of delight across her body.

She trembled as he pulled the shirt back up to cover her shoulder, trailing his fingers along her skin.

"Are you chilled?" he asked softly, his hands barely touching her shoulders.

She was anything but chilled. His caress had started a fever of desire within her. How could that be? How could she want a man's touch so badly he made her tremble? How could he touch her in such a way she felt it long after the caress was finished? "No." Her voice came out in a ragged whisper, and she was afraid to say more than that one word.

Mack began brushing her hair again, smoothing it with his hand as he brushed, so he was constantly touching her shoulders and back. Each touch sent a shiver through her. "Your husband was wrong, Becca. You are not cold. You are a giving, loving woman. The right man will bring that out in you. When he does, you will unlock the passion you've hidden away."

"What makes you so sure?" She doubted his words, but was curious to know why he would think so. He was a man much experienced with women. She could learn from him. If she dared.

"The way your body responds to my touch."

She stiffened. "How do you know? We have not touched! We are not lovers. I am not one of your women of loose morals."

He continued brushing as if she hadn't spoken. "The way you look at me."

That was too much for her. She twisted around to direct a glare at him. "And just how do I look at you?"

"As a cat looks at the canary just before she pounces."

She could see by the way his mouth twitched that he was only teasing her, but this was one area she would not be teased about.

She narrowed her eyes at him. "The wise canary would not draw the attention of the cat, because she has very sharp claws. Don't tempt her to sharpen them on you."

"Maybe that was not a wise choice of words." He studied her thoughtfully, tapping the brush against the palm of his hand.

"There is no *maybe* about it."

"It might be more correct to say the way you look at me is the way a starving woman might look if presented with a banquet table. Everything looks so good to her she can't choose which delicacy to try first."

Becca almost growled in frustration. "Mack, you are no delicacy, and this cat is about to pounce on the canary if you do not be quiet."

"I'm sorry, Becca, but I do enjoy teasing you. I'd rather see you angry than sad and then—" He stopped and firmly turned her head around so he could begin brushing her hair again.

"And then?" She turned back to study him. First he was playful, then mysterious, his mood so changeable she could scarcely keep up.

"And then it is better to tease you and talk about foolish things so I do not think about things I should not think about. That will only lead to me doing things I should not do."

She wrinkled her forehead as she tried to puzzle out his words. "Now you are talking in circles. Why can't you just say what you mean? First you must talk in riddles, and now you make no sense at all."

"I am talking in circles, for now we are right back to where we started." He stroked her cheek with the back of his hand. "If you truly do not want me to touch you, then you best stop looking at me the way you are."

"How am I looking at you?" She could barely concentrate on the conversation. His touch had confused her even more than his words. How could such a simple caress, just skimming along the surface of her skin, create such a myriad of confusing emotions?

"You look at me as if you want me to kiss you."

And he bent his head to hers.

He gently brushed his lips across hers, so quickly, she barely felt the caress before it was over. Becca sighed in surprise and delight. His lips were so soft and smooth, so firm and warm. She had never imagined what it would feel like for Mack to kiss her. She had never been kissed before.

Tilting her face up to him, she smiled, and he kissed her smile away, leaving her with another sigh on her lips as she swayed toward him.

He brushed his lips across hers once more.

Then, before she could object to the brevity of his kisses, his mouth covered hers again for just a heartbeat longer. When he kissed her again, she was ready for the touch of his lips, and she kissed him back.

As if that brief pressure was an unspoken signal, this kiss did not end as quickly as the others. Mack pulled her gently into his arms, increasing the pressure and intensity of his kiss.

Becca melted against him, her mind no longer able to think as sensation took over. As he teased the seam of her lips with his tongue, she opened her mouth to him. His tongue caressed and tasted her, and she clung to him as a wave of desire swept over her, making her weak and light-headed.

Her world shrank to the circle of his arms and the heat of him pressed against her. There was only the scent of pine and man.

When his kiss finally ended, it took Becca a moment to find the strength to open her eyes. She was half-afraid of what she would discover when she looked into Mack's eyes. Would he be disappointed? Would he laugh? When she met his gaze, she was reassured by the tender way he looked into her eyes.

He traced the sensitive flesh of her lower lip with the pad of his thumb. "That, my sweet Becca, is why you should not look at me the way you do. 'Tis too dangerous for us both."

She was still finding it difficult to control her breathing, especially with his arms still around her and his lips so close to hers.

She wanted to kiss him again.

She wanted.

Remembering the feel of his touch on her lips, she ran her finger across his mouth. "Maybe I am learning that I like danger."

"Becca, you do not know what danger is." He groaned against her mouth as she leaned forward to kiss him, but he did not push her away.

This time there were no featherlight kisses, only deep, hot tastes that left her body humming sweetly with pleasure when they finally stopped for air.

She nuzzled his cheek as she cuddled against his chest. "Yes, I find I do like to live dangerously, but fail to see what is so dangerous about kisses."

"The kisses are not so dangerous; the danger lies in what comes after." His voice was rough, but his hand gentle, as he stroked her hair.

"Riddles again, Mack? You've already made my head spin. After kissing you I can hardly think let alone solve a puzzle."

He brushed his lips across her forehead. "It is balm to my male pride that your head spins after kissing me, but it is hardly a puzzle what kisses lead to."

Giddy with pleasure, she wanted to tease a smile

back on his face. "I find I cannot solve even simple puzzles; maybe it would be best if you showed me."

He gave in to her request with a low groan, pulling her tight against him to kiss her long and hard. When his lips left hers to trace the column of her throat, she felt the flush of pleasure spread throughout her body, making her blood race hot and heavy in her veins. She wound her hands in his hair as he slowly parted the shirt she wore and shaped his hands around her breasts.

Waves of desire shimmered over her, and she let her head fall back as his hands and lips traced erotic patterns across her skin. He gently laid her back on the bedding. The rough wool blanket scratched her back, creating a sensuous contrast to the slick satin of his mouth.

She wanted that mouth on hers.

She wanted . . .

She did not know what she wanted.

"Mack, please . . . I want you." She guided Mack's mouth back up to hers and drank deeply of him as he leaned over her.

"I want you, too, sweet Becca. I've dreamed of this." His lips moved to the shell of her ear. He teased her with the tip of his tongue, making her writhe beneath him. He leaned more heavily upon her as he kissed her again, but as his tongue tangled with hers, all she could feel was the sweet sensation of his hands as they caressed her nipples to tender buds.

Then his hands moved lower to spread her thighs, and Becca froze for a moment as her body made the swift transition from pleasure to panic.

Rough hands, fingers digging into soft flesh. The smell of sweat and dirt and blood as he plunged between her thighs. Shattering pain. The warm ooze of blood between her thighs as he pulled away. The cold floor beneath her back when he finally left her alone, curled into a ball, weeping.

As her memories overcame the pleasure she had experienced only moments before, Becca bucked and fought, scratching and biting and shoving until the heavy weight that lay on her moved away and she was left panting and alone.

She pulled the shirt tight around her and wrapped her arms beneath her breasts, huddling on the blankets as she gathered her strength for the next attack.

"Becca!"

The sound of a male voice crying her name made her whimper, but she turned toward the sound, knowing it was better to see the subsequent assault coming so she could brace herself.

But the man crouching several feet away was not Hugh. It was Mack. The bewildered expression on his face struck at her heart, but it was the sight of the vivid scratch marks on his face that made her turn away.

Relief washed over Mack when he saw recognition light Becca's eyes. The transformation from willing lover to ferocious wildcat had been terrible enough, but the overwhelming fear in her eyes that blanked out everything but the urge to defend herself had shaken him to the core.

She had fought like a berserker, not caring what she did to vanquish the enemy. He could sympathize with that emotion, but did not like the idea that she saw *him* as that enemy.

Despite the burning scratches on his face and the taste of blood in his mouth from the lip she had split with her fist, the need to comfort her was nearly overwhelming. The small, whimpering noises she made after he left her alone tore at his heart. Wary, though, he did not go to her.

She lay quite still, the only movement her heaving chest as she gasped for breath, but he wasn't going to risk coming closer until he understood what had just happened between them. "What was that about?"

She turned back to face him, her eyes wide in her pale face, the only color two bright spots of crimson on her cheeks. "You frightened me."

She spoke so softly he could barely hear her, and it took a moment longer for him to understand what she had said. His worry disappeared beneath a wave of anger.

"I frightened you? Just what was it you were frightened of?"

"What you were trying to do." She struggled to a sitting position, not an easy accomplishment when she kept her arms wrapped around herself as if she expected him to rip the shirt off her at any moment.

He didn't like feeling like a rapist, especially when she had been the one. . . .

He ran his fingers through his hair. "If you didn't want to do that, then why did you tell me you did?"

Her eyes widened. "I never said I wanted that. All I asked for was kisses."

He reined in his temper, keeping his voice level. "I warned you what kisses lead to, and you wanted more. You said you wanted me. What was I supposed to think? My God, woman, you practically crawled into my skin; what was I supposed to do?"

Her breath hissed in. "I didn't know."

She looked so frightened, so innocent, he felt his anger slowly ebbing away, but not his resolve to get to the bottom of this. "What didn't you know?"

"I didn't know what I was asking."

"But you were married and the marriage was consummated. The proof of it lies over there." He waved a hand at Caroline's sleeping form. "How could you not know?"

She shook her head as she hugged her knees to her chest. "It was the kisses that did it. I didn't know what it meant to be kissed."

"What do you mean?" The last of his anger disappeared in his confusion. She was telling the truth. She truly hadn't known. He remembered the innocence of her first kisses and touches, until he had pushed her further than she was prepared to go. All she had needed to do was tell him to stop, but knowing her history, he could understand very well why she hadn't tried that route.

From everything he was learning of her husband, Hugh Wallace wouldn't have been stopped by a simple "no." She would have needed to fight him, which had surely gained her nothing but a few more bruises to nurse when it was all over.

But that still didn't answer the question of why she would lead him on, ask him to make love to her, when the very idea of it frightened her half to death. "Talk to me, Becca. Help me understand."

She bit her lip and looked at her daughter for a long moment before answering. "My husband used my body, but he never touched me the way you do, Mack. I've never been kissed before."

She gave him a weak smile. "You are a very good kisser, Mack. I should have listened to your warnings, but what I said earlier was true. Your kisses made me light-headed. I wasn't thinking straight. But that is no excuse. I am sorry I hurt you. You didn't deserve that."

He didn't deserve her. He had pushed her. He had rushed her. He had tried to make love to her and frightened her terribly. He was no better than his father.

No. He was worse than his father. His father's biggest sin had been neglect. Mack's offense was much worse than that. "I did, for being a fool, if nothing else. I should have known better, even if you did not."

"I'll clean out those scratches and put something on them to take the burn out." She stood, her legs still shaky, but the fear was gone from her eyes.

That was something at least. Mack thought he would do just about anything to keep that fear from coming back. Even if it meant never touching her again.

When she stretched her hand toward him, he flinched back. "No! I can do it myself."

Tears filled her eyes. "Mack, don't be that way. Please, don't."

"What way?" He clenched his hands into fists with the effort it took to keep from holding her in his arms.

"Don't hate me. Don't pull away from me. I know I hurt you, but please believe I won't do it again."

"I know that. I won't put you in that position again. I don't want you to be afraid of me."

"I'm not afraid of you, Mack."

"Maybe you should be."

CHAPTER 9

He held himself still as she smiled and reached up to touch his mouth with her forefinger. "How can I be afraid of you, when you've proven time and again, you will protect me—even from myself."

She was standing too close to him. He wouldn't have to take a step to hold her in his arms, to kiss her, to. . . .

He ground his teeth and prayed for strength before answering. "You were afraid only a few moments ago."

"I know, but I wasn't thinking. If I'd been thinking, I would have known you weren't going to hurt me." She traced the red scratches she had left on his cheek, catching her lip between her teeth.

Did she know what that gesture did to him? It made him want to capture that ripe mouth with his, ravish those lips with his teeth. He forced his gaze away from her mouth.

"Even when I struck out at you, you didn't hurt me. I know now that I can trust you. I won't forget that lesson. I won't be afraid again."

He deliberately put more weight on his wounded leg. The throbbing pain gave him focus and helped him keep his hands off Becca. "You would be afraid if you knew how close I came to taking you there, on the ground, while you screamed in fear."

"But you didn't, and that is all that counts. Next time—"

"There won't be a next time, Becca. I promise you that." He didn't know how he would find the control to move away from her, but he would find it. Somehow.

She smoothed her hand across his chest, leaning even closer. "I don't want that promise, Mack. I want you to touch me. I want you to kiss me. I want you to hold me."

Her lips trembled, so close to his it took every ounce of concentration to keep from leaning forward and tasting them.

He had never wanted a woman as much as he wanted Rebecca Wallace. Hell, he had never wanted anything as much as he wanted Rebecca Wallace. And he could not have her. Now, if he could only convince his body of that.

"No." His leg ached from the pressure of his weight on it, and he was grateful for the pain. It was a welcome distraction from another ache, slightly higher and centered between his thighs.

Tears filled her eyes, and she backed away. He clenched his fingers to resist the urge to hold her and comfort her. He knew that comfort would lead to something more, something dangerous.

Swiping the tears away with the back of her hand, she narrowed her eyes at him and raised her chin to a familiar stubborn angle. "Why?"

"Why?" His mouth went dry, and he couldn't think.

She put her hands on her hips. The movement left the shirt she wore gaping open. His shirt. The shirt he had unfastened to touch her.

The taut peaks of her nipples caught the material and held it at a tantalizing level, exposing the round curves of her breasts. He had caressed those breasts, teased those nipples with his tongue, only moments before. He ached with the need to touch her again, but knew he couldn't. What were his reasons for resisting? He couldn't remember.

A slow, sensuous smile curved her lips, and she gave him a knowing look as old as Eve and the Garden of Eden. "You don't know why, do you?"

"I know why," he insisted stubbornly. He knew there were reasons. He just hoped they would come to him quickly. And they better be damned good reasons.

She took a step closer to him. The scent of roses and woman enveloped him. His body hardened with the knowledge that her softness was so near.

She traced the line of his jaw. "Mack, you are so sweet, so noble. You want me. I know that. I can see it in the way you look at me."

"How do I look at you?" His voice sounded hoarse and raw.

"As if you want me to kiss you." She threw his words back at him.

Winding her arms around his neck, she stood on her toes and kissed him.

Her mouth was hot and sweet. He lost himself in those moist depths for a lifetime before he managed to pull back, but he couldn't escape far with her arms still around him.

His chest tightened until it was difficult to breathe. "That was not a good idea, Becca."

She kissed the corner of his mouth. "I think it was a very good idea. Kiss me again, Mack."

"Becca—"

She stopped him by laying a finger across his lips. "I need you, Mack. I need your help. I want to forget Hugh's touch. You can do that. I know that. You can banish the memory of his touch forever. Give me something good to remember."

That was not fair. If she allowed him to fool himself into thinking making love to her was a *good* thing, then he was done for. "Becca, you deserve more, better than I can give you."

The corners of her mouth twitched into a smile. "This from the man that was just telling me about the legions of women who will testify to his prowess."

There had been other women. He knew that, but he couldn't remember their names or their faces or their bodies. There was only one woman he wanted, but as much as he wanted her, there were things he wanted *for* her. "That is not what I mean. You deserve a husband, a better one than Hugh Wallace, and definitely a better man than me. You deserve a man who can love you.''

She slid her arms from around his neck as her smile faded. She gave him a thoughtful look. "You cannot love me?''

Maybe he was finally getting through to her. He could only hope.

"No." He had never needed to explain it to a woman before; the widows he had pleasured had understood the facts, but he owed Becca more. She was such an innocent in so many ways. There was so much she didn't understand. She deserved to know.

"That is why you won't take me, because you can't love me?''

"Yes.''

She smiled and pressed herself against him again. "Oh, Mack, you are the dearest man. I don't care a thimble for love. I don't believe in it. All I want from you is pleasure. I don't want you to love me; all I want is for you to make love to me. All I want from you is to help me bury the past. Can't you give me that?''

He wasn't sure he believed her, but a man could only withstand temptation for so long. With a groan he pulled her into his arms. He kissed her again, deeper and more urgently this time. He could do as she asked. He could love her so thoroughly, and so well, she would forget the bitterness of her past, and then she could move on.

And so could he.

Leading her to the bed of pine boughs, he pulled

her down beside him. Kneeling before her, he gently pushed the shirt off her shoulders. "You are so beautiful, Rebecca Wallace."

She smiled shakily. "I bet you say that to all your women."

He shook his head as he leaned forward to nibble at her lips. "It is not a seducer's lie, sweet Becca. It's only the truth."

"I am no beauty."

"Your skin is like cream, so white and smooth I could taste it forever." He skimmed his lips along her cheek and neck to graze her earlobe with his teeth.

He felt her shudder beneath his hands, and his body tightened with desire. He wanted her so badly he could push her back and take her now, but he would take it slow. He would give her what she wanted—a way to bury the past. "Your eyes are the deep, mysterious green of the forests. I could lose myself in their depths." He kissed her closed eyes and then tasted her mouth again.

As she opened to him, learning to answer the teasing dance of his tongue with hers, Mack knew he could not continue in this love play for long. But he had to make her desire him as much as he desired her. If that was possible.

"Do you still want this?" He drew back from her, gently stroking her jaw. "Are you certain?"

She raised her face to his, her lips swollen from his kisses, her eyelids heavy with passion. "I am certain."

"Then, undress me."

Her eyes widened, and her hands trembled slightly

as she placed them on his chest. She fumbled with the laces of his shirt as a flush of embarrassment pinked her cheeks.

As she pushed his shirt up, running her small hands across his chest, Mack groaned. She had touched him before, but only with the impersonal touch of a nurse. Now she was touching him as a lover, and it was nearly his undoing.

"Are you all right, Mack?" A pucker of worry appeared between her eyes. "Does your leg hurt too much?"

"What leg?" he teased her, kissing the worry line away. "The only pain I am suffering will soon be eased, unless you've changed your mind?"

When she shook her head, giving him a shy smile, he quickly pulled off his shirt. She moved into his arms without hesitation, the smooth warmth of her skin pressed against his chest as her mouth teased his.

Mack thought he might burst from wanting. He tried to concentrate on giving her pleasure. He caressed her breasts, stroking her nipples to hard peaks. He nibbled on her neck, sucked on her earlobe and teased the shell of her ear with his tongue.

But when she touched the laces of his buckskins, he almost lost control despite his best efforts. His breath hissed in as her fingers skimmed the hard length of him pressing against the laces.

"Did I hurt you?"

She was so innocent. He had to remember that she might not be a virgin, but she was an innocent when it came to the way things should be between a man and a woman. He must not frighten her.

"No, sweet. You do not hurt me, but sometimes pleasure can be so intense it is like pain."

"Will I help you with these?" She gestured at his laces.

It might be better for him if she did not; but with his wounded leg, he would need help getting his pants off, and it would give her one more opportunity to change her mind.

Heaven help him if she did, but he supposed he could spend the rest of the day in the cold spring water to find relief.

She helped him undress, her soft, quick hands touching him everywhere but the source of his need. She would not look at him either, fixing her gaze on anything but his rod.

When he was shed of his buckskins, he took her into his arms. She shivered slightly when her naked skin touched his, but she did not pull away. He tilted her face up to his. "Are you afraid, Becca?"

"A little, but I have not changed my mind." She tilted her chin at a defiant angle.

"I can understand your fear, and so I will let you be the one who has the power. I will not take you; you will take me."

Her eyes widened. "I don't understand."

"I will show you," he whispered against her mouth and kissed her again. Deepening his kiss until he felt her relax in his arms, he pulled her onto his lap, shifting her so her legs were spread wide and vulnerable across his thighs.

Her body stiffened slightly, but when his hands remained on her waist, she melted into his arms, winding her fingers through his hair. He smoothed his hands down the flare of her hips and her outer thighs.

She flinched slightly as he traced the length of her inner thighs to reach the soft, warm folds of her femininity. When his fingers began to stroke and tease her, her breath caught in her throat, and when he found the bud of her desire, she moaned against his mouth. As he stroked her, he was rewarded with the hot rain of her passion.

Her fingers dug into his shoulders as he slowly, rhythmically, probed her depths, and she whimpered against his mouth, kissing him hard. Suddenly, she tightened around his fingers as a tremor shook her body, and she cried out in surprise.

"Did I hurt you?" he whispered into her neck as he stroked her again.

He was rewarded when another tremor shook her body and she sighed against his chest.

"You did not hurt me, but I cannot say I understand what you did."

"I gave you the pleasure you sought."

"But . . . you did not . . ." She leaned back so she could study his face.

"No, I did not, but it is better for the woman, and truthfully for the man as well, if the woman is ready and willing."

"I told you I was ready and willing," she said softly, uncertainty in her voice.

"You were willing, but that is not the same as ready."

He teased the nub hidden within her moist folds, and she closed her eyes with a soft moan.

"Now you are ready."

He kissed her softly, tracing the line of her mouth with his tongue. "I want you, Becca, but you have to take me."

She opened her eyes again to search his gaze. "I don't know how."

"Touch me."

She placed her trembling hand on his chest.

"Lower."

She moved her hand down his chest, following the line of hair to his stomach and stopping as she looked at him.

"Take me into your hand, Becca."

He set his jaw as she closed her fingers around him. Just the touch of her hand was enough to give him release—if he let himself.

He curved his fingers around her hand and helped her guide his hard length to where her softness began. When the tip of his rod touched her, her eyes widened.

"You have only to move atop me and we will be joined, but it will have to be your move. You have the control, Becca."

And then the baby's wail cut through the silence of the clearing, followed by a dry rustle that struck fear through him.

Looking over Becca's shoulder, his worst fear was confirmed. A large timber rattler lay coiled in a spot of sun near the baby. The snake had probably lain there quietly for some time while he and Becca were occupied with each other, but now Caroline's rising cries and agitated movements were disturbing the snake. It began to shake its rattles in warning.

Becca nearly leaped from his lap and would have run to her child if Mack hadn't caught her and pulled her back.

"Don't keep me from her; she needs me." Becca struck out wildly, but he held her tight against his chest.

"You can't rush to her or the snake will strike out."

She stilled, her face white with fear. "What can we do?"

"Hand me the knife from my belt, but no more sudden movements, Becca."

Her mouth trembled, and tears filled her eyes; but her hand was steady as she gave him the knife. He fixed his gaze on the snake, slowly raising the knife. He didn't want to attract the snake's attention too soon. It would strike out in panic at the nearest threat; it wouldn't know the baby could cause it no harm.

Rising slowly to one knee, he still wasn't in a good position to throw a knife. He would rather be standing, but there was no time for that. He didn't want to disturb the snake any more than it already was. There would be only one chance. He said a quick prayer, aimed and threw.

CHAPTER 10

Mack's knife severed the snake's head from its still-twitching body. Becca scooped up her screaming baby with shaking hands.

Holding Caroline tight, she crooned in her ear to soothe her. "Hush, baby, everything's all right now. Mama's here. Nothing's going to hurt you while Mama's here."

The litany helped soothe mother as well as child. Caroline's cries of outrage subsided into hiccups as she mouthed Becca's naked shoulder. She squirmed in her mother's arms until Becca realized she was holding Caroline tighter than necessary.

Becca forced her fingers to loosen their grip so she could shift Caroline to her breast. The baby needed to nurse more than she needed comfort, even if Becca needed the comfort of holding her baby tightly in her arms and knowing Caroline was safe and well.

She focused on Caroline, checking the baby's fair skin for any marks, barely noticing when Mack carried the snake's carcass off into the bushes to dispose of it.

"She's okay, then?" Mack draped a shirt around Becca's shoulders.

She flushed in embarrassment as she hunched her shoulders to better cover herself. She had been so focused on her child, she had forgotten she was naked. But now, looking up at Mack, who was fully clothed again, she felt vulnerable and awkward. Only moments before they had been wrapped in the heat of passion, and now he looked so cold and distant, she wondered if she had imagined the whole episode.

It was easier to look at the baby and avoid Mack's gaze altogether. "She's fine. I don't know if she even noticed the snake. All she wanted was a full belly."

"That's all the snake wanted. There was a ground squirrel investigating the remains of our morning johnny cakes. I think the snake was after the squirrel, but it wasn't too happy about all the noise Caroline was making."

Becca shuddered. It would be a long time before she forgot the sight of the snake coiled and ready to strike. Her baby could be sickening or even dead by now if Mack hadn't been able to kill the snake before it struck. "Whatever he was after, I'm glad he's dead."

"So am I." For a moment, his eyes softened as he looked at the baby and reached out, as if to touch Caroline's downy curls, but then he turned away from them and moved to the fire. Lifting the pot of bubbling stew off the coals, he started kicking dirt into the fire. Within moments there was no hint of flame, and only the scent of smoke remained.

For the first time, Becca noticed the shadows were deepening around them. Soon it would be full dark. When Caroline had nursed her fill, Becca shrugged into the shirt and fastened it completely. Cuddling the drowsy baby against her shoulder, she moved to Mack's side. He still knelt beside the ring of stones where they built their fires, stirring the dirt with a stick as if to make sure there was no danger the fire would flare up again, his expression so distant she doubted he even knew what he was doing.

"Mack." She laid a tentative hand on his shoulder.

He flinched away from her touch and stood quickly to step away from her.

The sudden movement caused a twinge of pain to cross his face before he mastered his expression. "You better get dressed and gather your things while there is still enough light to see. We're moving out of here at first light. I don't want to spend much time breaking camp."

"Tomorrow?"

"Yes, tomorrow. We've lingered here too long as it is."

"But your leg, you're not rested—"

"If I'm well rested enough to make love to a woman, then I'm rested enough to take her to safety."

She winced at his harsh tone, not understanding how he could have changed so quickly from the lover who had wooed her so gently only moments before. "We're as safe here as we are anywhere. You've proven you're well enough to protect us. I trust you."

He gave a brief, humorless laugh. "Then, you're a fool, Rebecca Wallace. I'm the last man on earth you should trust with your safety. With luck, though, I should be able to keep my hands off you long enough to see you and your baby safely to Boonesborough."

Becca swayed in Joseph's saddle and watched Mack stumble again. This time he managed to catch himself before he fell. She winced in sympathy at the pain he must be suffering, but knew better than to say anything.

His wound was not healed, and his leg was still weak. He no longer walked with the easy grace she had admired before the Indian attack. But he had refused to ride Joseph and insisted he needed to be on the ground to watch for Indian sign. All she could do was make sure they stopped frequently so he could get some rest. "Mack, we need to stop soon so I can tend the baby."

He held up his hand, and she reined Joseph in.

Mack knelt and skimmed his hand just above the trail before staring down the narrow track that quickly disappeared into the forest. By the time he stood again, the forest had adjusted to their presence, and birds sang overhead while two squirrels chattered on a nearby stump.

Taking comfort from the normal sounds of the wildlife, she opened her mouth to ask him what he had found, but Mack gestured her to silence by laying a finger across his lips.

Standing stiffly, he limped back to her side. He waited to speak until he could put his hand on Joseph's neck. "A war party's been through here recently. Pretty big from the sign and moving fast. There's no telling how far away they are. I'd guess pretty far ahead of us, but I don't want to take any chances. Try to keep as quiet as you can. If Caroline starts squirming, let her nurse. We can't risk her crying. And don't call out to me again unless you must. Understand?"

Becca nodded. She wouldn't take him to task for his sharp tone. She could only imagine the pain he was in, and she understood his worry all too well.

"Can we go on a bit farther before we stop? There's a cave up ahead I think we can use for the night. It's too small for a war party to use and just enough off the trail that most would pass it by without seeing it."

She was more concerned about Mack than Caroline just now. Her belly full from nursing only a short time before, her daughter was cuddled into the shawl Becca had used to tie the baby to her. The makeshift sling kept Caroline secure and allowed Becca to keep her hands free to handle the reins, or her gun, if necessary.

Caroline was fine, but Mack was another story altogether. His skin was pale beneath his tan, and the lines of tension on his face were a testament to the pain he was suffering. "We can wait until then, but what about you, Mack? I can walk for a while."

"Don't worry about me," he said roughly and turned away.

Don't worry about him. As if he weren't in danger of collapsing at any moment. Becca set her jaw and kicked Joseph into motion, even though the horse was already stepping out behind his master.

There was no need to guide the animal—Joseph followed Mack without any instruction from her—so Becca divided her attention between Caroline and Mack. She could see the effort each step cost Mack, and yet, he continued to move forward at a quick pace. Now he no longer wore his long rifle strapped to his back, but rather held it in his hands as he constantly searched the trees.

Watching Mack made her nervous. Those days spent by the spring had helped her put the violence of Hugh's death to the back of her mind and forget their danger for moments, even hours. Now she felt vulnerable. There was nowhere to hide, and her confidence in Mack's ability to stand much longer, let alone fight, was rapidly fading. She remembered all too easily, though, the braves they had encountered that day and how they would have killed Caroline and taken Becca captive.

For comfort, she tightened her grip on the long rifle that lay across her knees. She had killed once to protect her daughter. She was prepared to do it again. And Mack was still standing. For now.

Mack stopped just ahead of Joseph and held up his hand. She reined the horse in and watched Mack. He raised his head as if listening for something and stepped off the trail into the undergrowth, disappearing from view.

There was a brief thrashing in the bushes, and then all was still again.

Taking a deep breath and forcing her hands to stop trembling, Becca fought back the urge to panic as she slid from Joseph's back. She checked to make sure Caroline was still secure in the shawl-sling. Then, taking up the long rifle again, Becca made her way to the break in the greenery where Mack had disappeared. Not knowing what had happened in there, she didn't know what she could do, if anything, to help Mack. But she had to do something. She owed him too much to just go on and leave him to face whatever problem he had encountered. If she could. If something had gotten to Mack, it could be stalking her right now.

Standing on the path, she could see nothing but leaves and a tangle of vine when she peered into the forest. She strained her ears to listen for movement as Mack had moments before, but the only sound she heard was Joseph impatiently blowing and stamping behind her.

She was reluctant to step off the path, but didn't dare call out to Mack. Draping Joseph's lead over her shoulder so she could grip the long gun with both hands, she plunged into the forest.

She held her breath for the first two steps, concentrating on watching and listening for trouble. There was nothing. All was still. No birds sang. No squirrels chattered. The air hung heavy and thick, making it difficult to breathe. Her hands were slick on the gun.

Then a strong arm circled her waist, just beneath Caroline's bottom, and a brown hand clamped over her mouth before Becca could draw the breath to scream. Her captor lifted her from the ground and turned her so she faced another Indian. The second Indian was holding a knife to Mack's throat.

Suddenly remembering the long rifle in her hand, Becca jerked the stock back, striking her captor in the gut. Her effort was rewarded by a grunt of pain. He released her so quickly she stumbled to the ground. Caroline squealed in protest at her mother's sudden movements, but Becca didn't stop to comfort the baby.

She didn't see any more Indians, but she wasn't going to take any chances. She swung the barrel of the long gun up and took careful aim at the brave holding the knife.

"Let him go." She couldn't be sure the Indian spoke English, but she thought he would understand her intent easily enough. She bared her teeth into a feral grin. "Let him go, and I'll think about letting you live."

The brave relaxed his arm and leaned against Mack to whisper something into his ear. Mack shook his head, and suddenly the two men were laughing out loud, hanging on to each other as if they were the best of friends.

An exaggerated groan of pain from the ground behind her drew Becca's attention to the youthful Indian lying at her feet. When he saw her turn to look at him, he made a big show of cringing from her, which sent the other two men into gales of laughter again.

Fear spiked into anger. She didn't like being

laughed at, and she didn't find their joke amusing at all. "Mack, just what is going on here?"

Mack wiped his eyes and slapped his companion on the back. "There's no need to shoot. These are friends of mine."

"I gathered that," Becca said dryly. "Of course, it might have been friendlier not to scare the wits out of me. I almost shot them."

"That is what amused Big Fist to no end. That and the fact you put Otter in his place. Big Fist was thinking about doing the same, but didn't feel right about thumping a chief's son. Otter was feeling very important about being chosen for this scouting mission, and now he's been felled by a woman."

The big Indian, Big Fist she thought, called something out in his own language. The Indian on the ground, Otter, chuckled and then groaned loudly again.

Mack's lips twitched, but eyeing Becca's dark expression, he didn't smile.

Her shoulders ached from the strain of holding the gun at the ready, but she wasn't ready to relax yet. "What are they saying?"

Mack's lips twitched again, and he fidgeted with his rifle, not meeting her eyes. "I don't think you want to know."

"Maybe not, but I demand you tell me." Becca narrowed her eyes at him.

"If you insist, but don't say I didn't warn you." He shrugged. "They said, 'Fire Woman will make a good squaw and she will make her husband very happy.'"

"That doesn't sound so bad." She studied him,

noticing the way he couldn't quite meet her eyes and the fact that Big Fist kept slapping him on the back. "What else?"

"They say a strong woman like you will breed up many strong children."

Becca shrugged. "And . . ."

"Well, the rest of it isn't important."

Maybe not, but the fact he wouldn't tell her seemed pretty important to Becca. "Mack, do I need to remind you I'm still holding a gun?"

He flashed her a quick look before turning his attention back to his rifle. "You wanted to know, so don't blame me. They think you are my wife, so they asked me if your hair is that same shade of red all over. They've had quite a debate over that. They concluded it must be, and therefore you have as much spirit in bed, thus making your husband a very happy man."

Becca set her teeth so she wouldn't smile. It was funny, but she didn't think she should encourage these men. They seemed to regard Mack as a good friend, and he was obviously not afraid of them; but that didn't mean she was ready to be so familiar with them.

Mack obviously took her silence for disapproval and shifted uneasily. "You must understand the Shawnee have a very bawdy sense of humor. They mean no disrespect. They especially will not offer any offense to the woman they believe to be my wife. That is why I did not correct them about that. I thought to offer you that protection at least."

Becca was enjoying his unease. It seemed some sort

of recompense. She decided to take the Shawnee's very personal question and use it to further torture Mack. "What did you tell them?"

"Tell them?" He looked at her in confusion, meeting her gaze for the first time.

She schooled her face into a blank expression. "How did you answer their question?"

He scowled at her. "I'll get the horse. We're camping here for the night."

Mack quickly moved past her, but not before she saw something she never expected to see on the frontiersman—a flush of embarrassment.

Becca ended up cooking dinner for the four of them. Luckily the Indians supplied a deer they had brought down before abducting the two whites. There was just enough corn meal left in Joseph's packs to make corn dodgers to go with the venison steaks.

It was an awkward evening with Becca cooking and serving them while the men whispered among themselves and laughed loudly at jokes made in a language she didn't understand. After they ate, the Indians' mood turned serious. She couldn't understand a word that was said, but she understood Mack's body language easily enough.

Whatever they had to say, it wasn't good news.

The men talked long into the night. Becca took Caroline off to one side and nursed her. She then made a pallet and lay down to try to sleep, but lay awake listening to the rise and fall of the men's voices.

Finally, Mack left the other two and joined her on the pallet. He sat down beside her, not touching her and yet so close she could feel the heat from his body.

"I should lie with you if they are to believe we are man and wife."

She smiled into the darkness. "We've slept beside each other for many nights. What is one more?"

"I thought things might be different now. . . ."

Things were different. She knew that even if she did not understand it. Something had made Mack pull away from her. Something had made his eyes turn cold. Something she didn't understand at all.

"Lie down, Mack. It will be all right," she said in a soft voice she normally reserved for her daughter. She only hoped she wasn't lying.

CHAPTER 11

"There's been a change in plans." Mack tightened his jaw, refusing to look at Becca. It was easier to concentrate on repacking Joseph's saddlebags. He wanted her too much to be easy around her.

"You don't look very happy about it," Becca said softly, moving closer to him. The early morning mist still hung low over the valley, so it seemed they were alone in the world, even though Big Fist and Otter were only steps away.

She touched his arm in an obvious attempt to make him look up. He shifted away from her touch. He refused to meet her eyes, but he couldn't escape the soft, sweet aroma of roses. The scent haunted his dreams.

"Happy?" He buckled the last pack closed and stood, wincing at the pain in his leg as he slung the pack over his shoulder. "You want me to be happy?"

"Yes. You deserve to be happy, no matter what you think, but that was not my point." She moved directly into his path, her hands on her hips and her chin at a determined angle. "What is wrong?"

"What is wrong?" He shook his head and gave her a mocking look. "Are you simple, woman?"

Her eyes narrowed, but she did not back down. "No. I am beginning to think you might be, though. Stupid and surly. That is not a very charming combination, I'll tell you."

"Maybe I'm not trying to be charming."

"So why don't you try being honest, then, and tell me what is wrong."

"What is wrong . . . Let's see." He rubbed his chin thoughtfully. "What could be wrong? I'm out in the wilderness with a helpless woman, a crying baby and a lame leg. I'm surrounded by Shawnee war parties. I need to get to Fort Boonesborough so I can get rid of the woman and the baby, but it would be suicide to run that gauntlet with such encumbrances."

"So why not just go on alone?" She wrapped her arms around herself. "If we are too much trouble, then why not leave us?"

She looked so small and alone. As if he could leave her behind. As if he had a choice in the matter. He ground his teeth together. "I can't. I promised I wouldn't leave you. I always keep my promises."

Painful memories flashed through his mind. His mother's frozen, bloody fingers reaching for his baby brother's broken body. His little sister's wide, staring eyes as she lay curled around her worn rag doll.

Forcing those memories to the dark recesses of

his mind, he focused on Becca. He would keep his promise to her if it was the last thing he did. He would protect her with his life. He would never make such a costly mistake again. Failure was not an option.

"You don't need to keep this promise. I release you from it." She straightened her shoulders and turned away from him.

He grabbed her shoulder and spun her around to face him again. Touching her was a mistake. His mind knew there could never be anything between them, but his body hadn't accepted that fact. Heat sizzled between them despite the chill morning air. Desire flared in him. Her eyes widened in surprise, so he knew she felt it, too.

He backed away from her, locking his gaze with hers. He couldn't afford to touch her again, but he had to make her understand. Touching her living warmth strengthened his resolve. She was alive, and he was going to keep her that way. "It is *my* promise. You cannot release me from it. I will not leave you behind."

"Why?"

"You don't need to know." She needed to know that he meant to keep his word, but he was not about to allow anyone, not even Becca, to see into that dark, tormented part of his soul.

"*Yes* I do." She took a step toward him.

He couldn't back away from her, even though he knew he should. She was too close—close enough to tease his senses with her scent, her heat. . . .

"Why?" He turned her question back on her. "Why do you need to know?"

"My life, and more importantly my daughter's life, depend on you. I need to understand the man I've put my trust in. Because I do trust you, Silas McGee."

"*That* was your first mistake."

Anger flashed in her eyes. "No. My first mistake was believing you were different from other men, but you are all the same. All that matters is your damnable pride. You don't care about me or Caroline. All you care about is your promise, so you can stuff your promise and . . ."

"And what? What will you do? You are in the middle of a wilderness in case you hadn't noticed. You are in danger. Don't you care about your skin, or Caroline's?"

"I think the real question is, do you?"

"Yes!" he shouted at her, making Big Fist glance up curiously from where he sat by the fire playing with the baby.

She gave him a small, satisfied smile. "So what do we do?"

That smile irked him. "Are you asking me? The same man who has led you into this disaster? The same man who will most likely get you killed tomorrow or the next day?"

"Yes. I am asking you." She laid her hand on his arm. "The same man who has saved me and my daughter more than once. The same man who has brought me safely through thus far. I believe in you."

"Then, gather your belongings and your baby. We're heading out, but not to Boonesborough."

She didn't even ask him why or where. She just did

as he asked. That show of trust shook him more than his need. He wondered which was the bigger mistake.

Mack cursed every step he took that day. They traveled from sunrise to sundown and made a cold camp with nothing but dried venison and corn to eat. His leg ached, and his stomach growled; but nothing compared to the knowledge that he was leading Becca and Caroline into danger—and he wasn't sure he could keep them safe.

He had thought after that afternoon at the spring, when they almost made love, that things couldn't get worse. He had been wrong. Though that night had been torture, he had managed to get through it knowing that the next day they would be moving toward Boonesborough, where he could say good-bye to one Rebecca Wallace.

He should have known things couldn't be that simple.

Meeting up with Big Fist and Otter had cost him another two nights on the trail. They had seen how weak he was and insisted on watching his back while he spent another day healing.

That meant two more nights spent sleeping beside Becca. Two more nights spent wanting her. Two more nights when she was close enough to touch. And then things got worse.

Even though Boonesborough was only a day's journey away, he was taking Becca and Caroline to Cutright's Station, and that destination added to their

time spent on the trail. Two more nights with temptation. But he had no choice.

He just couldn't be certain he had made the right
decision. Sure, Otter and Big Fist had scouted the
area enough to know a run into Fort Boonesborough
would be dangerous at best and nearly impossible
with a woman and child in tow. The pair of Indian
scouts weren't all too sure they could make it in to
warn the settlers without getting killed by one side
or the other, but they had been willing to take on
that task for Mack.

Which left him with one choice to get Becca to
safety—Cutright's Station. And that meant there was
no end in sight for his torture. He wouldn't be able
to hand over responsibility for her any time soon.
Keeping his promise would be the hardest thing he
had ever done, and it was further complicated by his
feelings for Becca.

It hurt just to look at her and know he couldn't
have her, but neither could he stop looking. Becca's
hair gleamed like the sunset in the soft blaze of the
fire. From Mack's position on the far side of the fire,
he could hear her soft humming as she soothed the
baby to sleep.

Damn, but he wanted her. That summed up his
situation perfectly. He wanted her. He was damned.

He was damned three times over. He was damned
because he wanted her. He was damned because he
had made her want him. He was damned because he
had made her trust him.

He lay back against his rough blanket and stared
up at the expanse of stars overhead. The night sky

was so clear and dark, the stars seemed so close, he could nearly reach up and touch them.

"Mack, where are we going?"

The scent of roses surrounded him as Becca knelt on the edge of his blanket. She laid Caroline on the pallet beside her. The baby made small sucking noises in her sleep.

It was easier not to look at her. Not much easier, but enough, maybe. "Cutright's Station."

"Why Cutright's Station and not Boonesborough?"

As she asked, she reached for the bandage on his leg. He slapped her hand away without looking. His wound was healing well enough as far as he could tell, and he couldn't afford her touch. Every time she touched him, every time she was near, the temptation grew stronger, and his ability to withstand it grew weaker.

Two more days. Tonight and then one more. He had only to make it that long. He could make it that long. He hoped. "Too many war parties around Boonesborough. We couldn't get through."

She touched his cheek. "Mack, please look at me."

Shaking off her touch, he ground his teeth as he fought for control. He could still remember the black timber rattler coiled to strike beside Becca's helpless baby. He had let down his guard to make love to the mother and almost cost the child her life. That was what happened when Mack dared to reach for happiness. He would not make that mistake again. But that resolve didn't stop the wanting.

Damn, but he desired her. He couldn't remember ever wanting a woman so much. And that might cost her everything. He owed her that much truth. "My luck has turned. If I were you, Becca, I would take my daughter and run as fast and as far away from me as you can get. At the least, stay more than an arm's length away. The other side of the camp might be safe enough—for now."

She shook her head, the firelight glinting off her curls. "I think not. I'm not running away. I trust you more than luck, Mack."

"You shouldn't."

"What has happened to us?"

The wistful note in her voice tore at his heart. "Nothing has changed. I am your protector. That is all. Do not make the mistake of thinking there is more to this than that."

Her breath hitched. "I have not. I know when you have taken me to safety you will be done with me. But I thought until then . . ."

"You thought what?" he demanded harshly.

"I thought you wanted me."

When she reached for him, he flinched away. "I did." That much was the truth. He had wanted her. Just as he wanted her still, but it was best if she didn't know that. He hoped putting it in the past tense would send the message without making him lie. He didn't want to lie to her. Just looking at her was torment, so he focused on Caroline, stroking the baby's petal-smooth cheek with his finger.

"Who is at Cutright's Station?"

Looking from the baby to Becca, Mack couldn't make any sense of her question. "What?"

"Who is she?"

"She?"

"Stop repeating everything I say. Who is she?"

"There are only three *shes* at Cutright's Station. There is Ruth, my friend Cutter's former slave. There is Ima, his baby girl. And there is Emily, his wife."

Becca gave a small sigh. "It is Emily."

"Emily? What does she have to do with anything?"

"She is the reason you won't touch me or as much as look at me, isn't she?"

He thought briefly of confirming her suspicions—after all, he had once asked Emily to marry him—but he quickly discarded the idea. The two women would meet soon enough, and Becca would learn the truth. "Emily doesn't have anything to do with anything. She's my friend's wife and that is the end of it."

"Something has happened. Something has come between us, and I need to know what."

"You need to know?" His body tensed as he watched her carefully. "You need to know?"

"Yes." She lifted her hand toward him and then obviously thought better of touching him and let it fall to her lap.

He flashed a hard look at her. "Wrong. You don't need to know any such thing. I thought you trusted me?"

"I do."

"Then, trust me to know I've made the right decision." He hated using her trust as a weapon, but he had no choice. "You are better off."

Her eyes sparked in anger. "Maybe you think you are better off."

The sign of her passion touched off an answering spark in him, and he buried it quickly. Bracing himself, he touched her to remind himself of the feel of warm, living woman, to remind himself of the contrast, of what could happen if he didn't keep his promise.

"You are better off, Becca. Remember that. Now go to your bed and sleep. I will watch over you."

She picked up her sleeping child. Resting her cheek against the top of Caroline's head, Becca gave him a searching look. "And who will watch over you, Mack?"

CHAPTER 12

Becca curled around her sleeping daughter. After another long day on the trail, she should be exhausted, and she was, but still she couldn't sleep. She sensed Mack's eyes on her. He was watching her again. Just as he had been observing her all day. She couldn't make a move or draw a breath without him taking note. He was making her daft.

Maybe madness was catching. For surely Mack had caught some illness of the mind. Ever since they had left the spring, he had acted half cracked, and she never knew what he would do next.

No. That wasn't true. There were certain things she could predict with ease. She knew that if she moved too close to him, he would move away. She knew that if she touched him, he would pull away. She knew that he had not willingly touched her since that day.

And that was making her crazy. Maybe it was catching.

Two weeks ago, if she had even dreamed that she would want a man's touch this badly, she would have wondered about her sanity. But that was before she had met Mack. Before he had touched her with gentle hands and rough lips. Before she had learned that a man's touch did not always bring pain.

Unless you counted the ache in her heart.

"Mack?" She knew he would answer her. He wouldn't touch her, but he hadn't begun ignoring her altogether.

"Go to sleep, Becca. We will start out early tomorrow morning so we have a hope of reaching Cutright's Station before nightfall."

"I can't sleep. Won't you talk to me?" She rolled on her side to face him across the fire pit where the coals from their cook fire still smoldered.

"I'm talking, ain't I?"

"I mean really talk. As in conversation. Tell me what you are thinking. You used to talk to me."

He gave a short, humorless laugh. "You make it sound like we've known each other forever. It's only been just over a week since we met."

"And you're sorry for it, aren't you?"

She could hear his sigh from across the clearing.

"Go to sleep, Becca."

She cupped her baby's cheek, drawing comfort from the sweet warmth of her child, comfort and courage. She had always been able to draw courage from Caroline before, but then, she had never really wanted anything for herself until now.

"Maybe it would have been better if we'd never met."

"How would that be better? Most likely if I hadn't come across you and the baby in the woods that night, you'd both be dead by now. Dead or taken captive."

"It would be better for you. You say your luck has changed. I think it's my fault. I've never had much luck myself, and it seems everyone I've ever come close to has bad luck, too."

"No." He sat up from his blanket. "It was their bad luck not to treat you the way you deserved."

"What do I deserve?" she asked softly.

"What do you want?"

Unable to meet his direct gaze, she looked away. Staring up at the night sky, Becca suddenly felt overwhelmed. For so long she had concentrated on just keeping alive to protect Caroline. She had thought only about what she wanted for Caroline. She had never imagined she would have the opportunity to have something for herself.

And the only thing she wanted was Mack, but she wasn't ready to admit that to him yet. "I don't know what I want."

"You need to learn to dream."

"What do you dream about, Mack?"

He was so quiet, she thought he was going to ignore her question.

"I dream about peace."

"For yourself?"

"For all of us. Some day I hope not to have to take care of someone else, to look out for someone else, to worry about anyone but myself."

She bit down on her lip in an effort not to cry. She had known she was a burden to him, but she had thought he took it on gladly. "Wouldn't you be lonely?"

He laughed again. There wasn't any humor in the sound. "Do you know how lonely it is to be the one who must always look out for others? It is a very lonely life, Becca, when everyone looks to you to watch out for them."

"Like me?" She wanted him to tell her she was different, but she knew better.

"Like you," he agreed.

She hugged her knees to her chest and ignored the aching pain in her heart. "Then, it would have been better if you hadn't found me that night."

Her throat tightened painfully until she could barely speak. "It would have been better if you let Hugh kill me or the Indians take me. It would have been better if I died."

Hot tears trickled down her cheeks, and she turned her head so he couldn't see her cry. She wanted him, and he saw her only as a burden. If it wasn't for her daughter, she would have wanted to die in truth.

And then his arms were around her. "Oh, sweet Becca, don't cry. I didn't mean to make you cry."

"I'm not crying." She drew in a ragged breath and kept her face buried in her hands so he couldn't see her tears. She didn't want him to see her weakness. She had that much pride left.

He gently pushed her hands away from her face. Cupping her face between his hands, he kissed her

tears away. "I won't let anything happen to you. I
made a promise and I always keep my promises."

"Do you?"

"Yes."

"You didn't keep the promise you made to me at
the spring."

"What promise was that?"

"You promised you would help me bury the memory of the pain that Hugh caused."

Something flashed in his eyes. She thought it might
be fear, but she knew better than that. Nothing frightened Mack.

"I did, didn't I?" His voice was flat, emotionless,
all sign of tenderness gone.

He didn't want her, then. It was that simple. He
hadn't really wanted her before. That had been
merely a simple case of having no choice. She had
been the only woman around, but tomorrow there
would be a choice.

"Maybe it would have been better if I'd never been
born."

"Never think that. Never." Gripping her shoulders,
he gave her a little shake to emphasize his point.

She was surprised at the violence of his protest.
Surprised enough to forget her misery for a moment.
"Why?"

"Because then Caroline would never have been
born." He touched the sleeping baby's head. "As
much trouble as she can be at times, I think the world
would be a sadder place without her."

He tilted her chin up to meet his gaze. "Just as it

would be a sadder place without you, Becca. I am glad to have the chance to know you.''

"Even if I have been a lot of trouble.''

"Even if." He traced the curve of her jaw with his hand. "You have made my life better for knowing you. Your life has meaning and don't ever forget it.''

"I won't." She touched his cheek gently and gave him a small smile. "You are a man of contrasts, Mack. I never know what to expect from you.''

"That is the way I like it.''

"But one thing is constant. You are always gentle with me.''

He froze. "I am not a gentle man. You should know that by now. You've seen me kill.''

She closed her hand over his. "I know you are not a gentle man, but you can be gentle. That is all that matters to me.''

"Don't.''

He tried to pull his hand away, but she clung to him with all the determination she possessed in her small body. "Don't what?''

"Let me matter to you. That can only lead to trouble, Becca.''

"Too late," she whispered.

"Don't care about me.''

Hope flared within her. He sounded so forlorn. He did not want the lonely life he talked about. She could feel it in the way he touched her, in the way he watched her. But she would have to take the first step to tear down the wall he had built between them. "It is too late for that. It was too late the day you were wounded saving my baby's life.''

"That is what I do. It doesn't mean anything."

And she saw a flicker in his eyes that told her she had been wrong. His desire for her hadn't gone away—not one whit. He had only kept it hidden. Why, she couldn't know. She would puzzle that out later.

"It means something to me." She leaned forward and kissed him; feather-light and quick, she brushed her lips across his.

He groaned and pulled her into his arms, kissing her deeply. She wound her arms around his neck, pressing so tight against him she seemed to feel his heart beating against hers. His hands traced the flare of her hips, the tuck of her waist and came up to cup her breasts. His lips left hers to trace the column of her throat and the swell of her breasts. He suckled the turgid points of her nipples through the thin muslin of her shift.

She felt the newfound rush of heat between her legs, and she lay back on the pallet, pulling him with her. This time the weight of a man on top of her created no panic and no fear—only desire. She knew what she wanted.

He helped her remove her shift, and she helped him with his breeches; and then he was moving his strong, lithe body across the length of hers. She ached for him to take her, but instead he teased her with his lips and hands.

"Mack, please!"

"I thought I was pleasing you." He nipped at her earlobe and teased the shell of her ear with his tongue.

She reached for him, kissing him hungrily. Now that she had him touching her, she never wanted to let him go.

"Love me, Mack. Love me, please."

She knew immediately she had said the wrong thing. His face was all shadows; only his eyes glinted in the faint glow of the embers. She couldn't read his expression, but she could feel the sudden tension fill his frame.

He pulled away from her, only a few inches, but she knew it might as well be miles.

"I told you before. I can't love you. I don't have it in me."

"And I told you before. I don't believe in it." But she knew he didn't believe her.

"You better get some sleep." He stood without looking at her again. "We leave at first light, and we won't stop until we reach Cutright's Station. We won't spend another night on the trail."

They left the camp in the predawn light. The only ones who got any sleep were Joseph the horse and baby Caroline.

They traveled hard all day, and as dusk crept over them with no station in sight, Becca thought she might just let exhaustion win. She swayed on Joseph's wide back and wondered if Mack would even notice if she fell to the ground in a dead faint.

He hadn't looked back at her all afternoon. He hadn't looked her in the eye all day and once again did everything possible to avoid touching her.

Despair overwhelmed her. Not even the squirming warmth of her baby, cradled against her body, could bring more than a fleeting glimpse at hope.

"Why have you stopped?"

Mack's voice at her side jolted her out of her stupor. She hadn't even realized Joseph had halted. She didn't really care. "I am so tired. I don't think I can go on."

"The station is just ahead. Don't give up now."

It might have been her imagination that his voice softened slightly. He did not touch her, simply slapped Joseph's flank to start the horse moving again.

True to Mack's word, within moments they left the forest and came into cultivated land. The sun had already gone down, but there was enough gray light left to sight the looming station walls. The gates stood open as a young man called in the cows for the night, and lights winked a welcome.

Then they were sighted, and the calm of the evening was shattered. She was too exhausted to notice more than a cacophony of sound—shouted greetings, barking dogs and the lowing of cattle—as Mack led them through the gates. A tall, stern man lifted her from her saddle, and a slender woman with the bluest eyes she had ever seen put her arm around Becca when her legs wobbled.

"Come. We'll get you inside." The woman's throaty voice was low and comforting as she spoke to Becca, but as soon as she settled Becca on a low bench inside the brightly lit kitchen filled with people, the woman turned on Mack with a hiss of anger. "What have you done to the poor girl? She is bone tired."

"I've done nothing but save her."

Even now, Mack wouldn't look at Becca. All his attention was focused on the other woman, and Becca knew this was Emily.

"Her husband was killed and her cabin burned. We were lucky to make it this far with our scalps. The Shawnee are on the warpath again."

CHAPTER 13

A shaft of sunlight worked its way through a chink in the stable wall and struck Mack across the face like a blow. He winced away from the light.

From the strength of the sun it was much later in the morning than he usually slept, but then it had been a hard journey. More than that, though, waking meant seeing Becca again—as if she hadn't haunted his dreams. Groaning at the thought, he covered his face with his arm to block the persistent sunbeam.

Little girl giggles bubbled over him, shattering the hope that he might return to the comfort of sleep. He opened his eyes to face his tormenter.

"Morning, Uncle Mack." Four-year-old Imogene Cutright knelt beside him wearing a pair of worn overalls obviously inherited from her older brother. A green ribbon that exactly matched the shade of her eyes strained to hold back her mane of brown

curls. Her green eyes danced at him as she covered
her mouth with her pudgy hands to stop more giggles
from erupting.

"Morning, darling." Mack managed to summon
up a smile for his friend's daughter. Normally, Ima's
sunny disposition was enough to bring a smile to his
face without effort, but not today.

"Mama told me to waked you up if'n you want
breakfast." She tilted her head as she studied him,
wrinkling her nose at him. "You might want to wash
up first. Yer a tad scruffy, Uncle Mack, and you smell."

After stretching, Mack gave her a deep bow. "I am
sorry to offend my lady."

"That's all right, but you know how Mama is about
washing." She leaned in, cupping her hand around
her mouth to whisper in his ear. "Make sure you get
the backs of yer hands, too. She checks those before
she lets you sit at the table."

"Thanks for the tip," he said gravely and allowed
her to escort him down from the loft.

As Ima towed him from the stable into the station
yard, his gaze fell on Becca. It worried him how drawn
he was to her. She sat on a bench, nursing Caroline,
with Emily Cutright and the freedwoman, Ruth, gathered around her. The women were laughing. He had
forgotten how beautiful Becca was when she laughed.
The sight tore at his heart, and he must have made
some sound.

Becca saw him first, and her laughter stilled immediately. She stood, handing Caroline to Ruth. "I had
best get back to work. I've dawdled enough."

Emily gave Mack a hard look and put her hand on

Becca's arm to hold her in place. "You've had a hard journey. You need to rest to recoup your strength."

"I'm as rested as I'm going to be. There's work waiting while I dawdle here."

She wouldn't look at him. Mack tightened his jaw. It was just as well for them to avoid each other, he knew that, but that didn't mean he had to like it. So he stood like a post, still holding Ima's hand.

"Nonsense." Emily squared her shoulders. "There is no need for you to do field work. If you feel you must work, you can stay here in the station and help."

"I thank you for your kindness, but that corn needs to be hoed, and I don't mind the work. I find it relaxing. You are both carryin' and can't be working in the fields, but I can if you'll just watch the babe. I best be going."

"Why?" Emily gave her a stern look.

Becca lifted her chin. "I've got to earn my keep."

"You need do no such thing," Emily said indignantly, her hands on her hips. "You are a guest here."

"I won't be a burden to anyone, thank you just the same, Mrs. Cutright. If you can watch over Caroline while I work, I'd be much obliged."

Emily waited until Becca had passed through the gates before whirling on Mack. "Silas McGee, you have a great deal to answer for. What have you done to that woman?"

"I've done nothing but save her life." And made her hate him, but that was none of Emily's business.

She narrowed her eyes at him. "And just what does she think she owes you for that?"

"Nothing. I've never told her that she owes me a thing for that debt."

Emily set her jaw in a familiar stubborn expression. "I am going to get to the bottom of this, you can count on that. And I dare say it does not reflect well on you."

Moving to the rain barrel so he didn't have to meet her angry gaze, Mack scooped water out to splash his face. "Marriage and motherhood hasn't softened you one bit, Emily."

"It hasn't made me go soft in the head, if that was what you hoped. My mind is as sharp as ever, and you better watch your step because my tongue is even sharper."

"I hadn't noticed," he commented dryly and headed for the kitchen in hope of finding something for breakfast. In her present mood, Emily certainly was not about to offer him anything but his head on a platter.

Emily followed him into the kitchen. "What have you against women that you must make them so miserable?"

He found some corn bread on the table and took a bite, watching Emily pace the room as he chewed. "There are some women at the fort who would gladly tell you I've made them quite happy."

"For a moment." She snapped her fingers beneath his nose. "And we both know there is more to life than that."

"Not if you do it right, Em." Taking his corn bread, he stepped back outside. He winked at her as she followed him back into the sunlight. "I'll have to give Cutter some tips."

Folding her arms, she gave him a smug smile. "My husband knows how to treat a woman, in and out of bed, which is more than I can say for you, Silas McGee. What is to become of that girl? Are you planning to marry her?"

"Why would I do that? Her husband's been dead little more than a week, and we barely know one another." Finishing his corn bread, he took a dipper of water from the well and drank deeply. "And you know I'm not the marryin' kind."

"You once asked me to marry you," she said quietly.

Mack grinned at her. "That was just to force Cutter's hand, and you know it. We wouldn't have lasted a week before one of us tried to kill the other."

"That's true enough, but Becca is a different sort of woman. She has feelings for you, Mack. What are you going to do about that?"

Unable to stop himself, Mack made his way to the gates to watch Becca in the field. She worked between Cutter's teenage son, Tad, and Ruth's husband, Reuben. The black man said something that made Becca smile and Tad laugh out loud.

"As soon as things calm down, I will take her to the fort, and you need not concern yourself about her," he said to Emily without taking his eyes off Becca.

"I will concern myself with her if I choose," Emily snapped at him. "And if you think it will be that easy to rid yourself of her, then you will be in for a big surprise."

"I am not looking to rid myself of her," Mack lied with great dignity. "I am merely looking out for her. I think it is best for her to go to the fort as soon as possible."

"And what does she think is best?" Emily asked pointedly. "What does she want? You know women are not pieces of wood you can move about at will. We have thoughts and feelings."

He was glad to see Cutter step from the trees. Usually Mack enjoyed arguing with Emily, but not today, and not about Becca.

His friend kissed his wife and turned back to look at the forest surrounding his cleared fields. "I've not seen any Indian sign, but then, I did not go very far from the clear.

"Come. I want to take a look around, unless you'd rather hoe corn?" Cutter didn't wait for him to answer, simply walked past him and disappeared into the forest.

Shouldering his rifle, Mack followed. He would rather face a horde of murderous Indians than skirmish with Emily some more. The men spent most of the day skirting a wide circle around the station and found no Indian sign, but neither man was comforted. They finally stopped beside the creek that ran along the Cutright's southern boundary.

Cutter set one foot upon a boulder and rested his long rifle across his knee, his green eyes scanning the trees and water. "I'd be happy to sell you a piece of land on the other side of this crick. It would be nice to have you as a neighbor."

Mack gave his friend a level look, not fooled for

one minute by the man's casual attitude. "You know
I've no mind to settle down."

"That's what you always said, but men have been
known to change their mind."

"I won't." He pressed his lips firmly together. Stephen Cutright was the closest thing he had to a
brother, but that did not mean he meant to tolerate
Cutright's interference in his life. It was bad enough
to hear it from Emily.

"So what do you mean to do about that girl and
her baby?"

"Why does everyone assume she's my responsibility?" Mack asked irritably. "I saved her; that was my
job. I was only doing my duty. Now I've seen her to
safety. Once I can safely deliver her to the fort, I'll
be done with her."

Cutter turned and gave him a long look. "I might
believe that if I hadn't seen the way you look at her."

"And how's that?"

"The way you shouldn't if you don't mean to make
her your wife."

Mack forced his fingers to loosen their grip on his
rifle. He wouldn't take a shot at Cutter as much as
he wanted to. For one thing, Cutter was his friend,
and more important, it was no sure thing he would
get off a shot before Cutter tried to cut him down.
Both those things shouldn't have required thinking
about. It frightened him more than a little to feel the
depth of the rage sweeping through him. He tamped
it down with great effort. "You used to look at Emily
that way and had no intention of marrying her. It

only took a troop of English soldiers and a Shawnee war party to make you see sense."

"So what will make you see sense?"

Mack narrowed his eyes. "Nothing will work for me, as I told your wife."

"You've certainly got her riled up, that's for sure."

"Then, it is a good thing we will not be neighbors."

Cutter gave him a measured look and then shrugged easily, turning back to his study of the trees. "Becca and her child are welcome to stay here as long as they like. There's no need for you to stay. As you can see, I've got things well in hand, and now that Tad is back home, we've got another gun if needed."

Cutter was right. Mack should go—now, before it was too late—but they both knew he was not leaving. Heaven only knew why he was so determined to stay when the best thing that could happen was another Indian attack. Better not to think too much about his reasons for doing anything of late. "Why is Tad home? I thought he would be still at William and Mary."

"So did we, but he is no longer a boy for me to order about. He only went to study for his grandmother's sake, and now that my mother is gone, there was nothing to keep him in Virginia. With the fighting all but over in the East, he thought we could use another gun here. It looks like he was right."

"He is so young."

"Not so young as all that. Many men marry by his age or about. Mayhap, he will take your young widow off your hands so you need not trouble yourself over her."

"Stop talking foolishness; he is just a boy." Mack ground his teeth just thinking about it. Unwilling to stand still any longer, he turned on his heel and headed back for the station.

Mack had good reason to remember his words when they arrived back at the cabins. Tad and Becca sat on the bench outside the kitchen with a bowl of string beans between them, but their heads were close together as he whispered something in her ear. Her eyes sparkling with delight, Becca laughed, tilting her head to display the long, white column of her throat.

Grinning widely, Tad watched her. The look in his eyes was far more appreciative than Mack liked. Cutter was right. Tad had grown up. But Mack was still the better man in a fight.

He tossed the rabbits he and Cutter had shot at Tad's feet. "Why don't you clean those up for Ruth and Emily. I'll help Becca finish these beans."

As Cutter and Tad moved off with the game, Becca tightened her mouth and concentrated on snipping the beans.

He watched her, but she did not look up. "You have settled in well enough, I see."

"Your friends are good people; they have been very kind to me." Her fingers flew over the beans, making quick work of the task.

"Then, do not repay that kindness by teasing their son."

Her forehead creased as she slid a quick look at him. "Teasing?"

"Your position is secure here. I have seen to that. There is no need to flirt with Tad."

Her fair skin flushed, and her eyes brightened. She picked up the bowl of beans, gripping the wooden rim until her knuckles whitened. "You do both your friends and me wrong with such a judgment. Yes, they welcome me for your sake, but also for mine. As I said they are good, kind people and would open their home to any stranger in need, I think, with no question of anything owed. I am no light-skirt who will pay her way in that manner."

Seizing her wrist to hold her in place when she would have swept past him, Mack leaned in close. "I agree with you about my friends, but question your description of yourself. It was *my* forbearance that kept you off your back on our journey, if you remember. You were willing enough."

Her breath hissed out through her teeth. "Do not count on such willingness again. I gravely misjudged you as a man because my standard of measurement was so low. Now that I have met men of a higher caliber, I shall not make that mistake again."

She twisted her wrist free of his grip, but he stood quickly and slid his arms around her waist. She still held the large wooden bowl in front of her, but he simply moved to her side, nuzzling her neck. She held her back stiff and resisting, but he felt the tremor that shook her as he tasted her skin with his lips.

He traced the shell of her ear with his tongue. "You want me still. Do not try to deny it." He traced the line of her face and ran the pad of his thumb across her trembling lips.

Her mouth parted.

He smiled at her.

She bit his thumb.

Cursing, he released her, and she stepped nimbly away, hurrying to the kitchen. Her hand on the door, she turned back. "Do not touch me again."

CHAPTER 14

Mack shifted his position on the watchtower, but could find no easy place to sit or stand. Usually, he was so in tune with his body, he could find a comfortable position with ease and keep it for hours on end as he watched for game or an attack. But not tonight.

It was a good thing he was keeping watch, more as a way to escape from Becca's company than out of necessity. There were hostile Indians ranging the Kentucky frontier, but it seemed none were drawn to the area surrounding Cutright's Station. At least he and Cutter had not been able to scare up any sign during their scouting, and if neither of them found sign, then there was probably none to be found.

Even so, Mack chose to keep watch in the tower Cutter had built atop his kitchen cabin. High enough to serve as a vantage point for the cleared land surrounding the station, it was more of a covered widow's

164 *Deanna Mascle*

walk; but the children had dubbed it a tower, and so the name had stuck.

His evening's watch had brought nothing more into view than a pair of deer come to nibble on the half-grown corn and a family of possum waddling along the edge of the forest on their way to the creek. But then, a whole tribe of hostile Indians could be camped against the edge of the walls where he could not see, because time and again his attention was drawn to the group gathered below in the station yard.

More accurately, his gaze was drawn to Becca. She sat beside the fire Emily insisted be set in the station yard despite the warmth of the evening.

"The children enjoy watching the fire, popping corn and roasting chestnuts, and we have cause to celebrate life tonight. After all, Mack and Becca have come safe through their trials." The look she gave Mack did not soften.

He got her message loud and clear. For him, the trials were far from over. He knew she was right.

Mack had spent many a night gathered around bonfires with the Cutright clan, but not tonight. Tonight he was keeping guard, knowing it was a futile gesture. *After all, how do you keep watch for the enemy within?*

There were worse things than spending an evening among friends gathered around a fire, popping corn and sharing songs and stories.

Mack knew there were worse things than listening to Becca's throaty laugh after Tad told one of his outrageous tales about Virginia society, watching her green eyes widen when Cutter described his adventures with the Indians and hearing her sweet soprano meld with Reuben's deep voice in a duet.

But he thought it might be easier to be tortured by the Cherokee, burned alive by the Shawnee, scalped by the Mohawk, or shot by the British than to struggle through this evening. At least then he knew his death would bring final release. Mack was certain there would be no such easy escape for him this time.

Damn, but she was beautiful. He wanted her more than he had ever wanted anything, and there was nothing he could do about it.

Despite her words earlier, he knew he could have her in his bed this very night, if he but asked. He could make love to her until the need had been burned out of him.

Maybe.

A belief had started in the back of his mind, a nagging doubt, that he might spend a lifetime making love to Becca and not burn the need for her from his soul.

For all that his eyes were drawn to Becca's every movement, and his ears to her every word, he noticed other things. He watched Reuben touch his hand to the swell of his wife's belly and Ruth's gentle smile as she covered his hand with hers. He saw Cutter slide his hand down the curve of Emily's breast when they thought no one was watching and the way Emily laid her hand on her husband's thigh.

More than the sure welcome, more than the confident love, Mack envied them knowing each would bed down beside his woman tonight and the next and the next. He had never wanted that before. Before Becca.

Once it had been enough, when the need grew great, to seek out a willing woman for a few hours. But now, he was afraid a few hours would not satisfy this urge.

And Mack did not like being afraid. He could resent Becca for that alone.

Turning his gaze back to her, he saw that she watched him quietly from across the fire. He turned his back so he did not have to see the hurt in her eyes.

Becca stood, careful not to wake Ima, whose small frame had slumped against her as she fell asleep. She eased the sleeping girl into a more comfortable position on the rag rug they shared to soften the hard ground.

Turning to Emily, Becca held out her arms for her own sleeping daughter. "Your arms must be about ready to fall off. My baby is no lightweight, I know, and you are not well used to holding such a weight for any length of time."

"But they must accustom themselves, for soon we will have two babes that need holding. I do not mind the practice." Emily smiled up at Becca as she relinquished the baby.

"I think it is past time I put her down, and I think I will find my own bed as well."

"You must be tired after spending a day in the field, but there will be no need for that tomorrow. Mack and I will take our turn with the hoe and shovel so you can stay in the station." Cutter rose from his seat with the lithe grace of a panther.

He gently caressed his wife's cheek with his knuckles, and she leaned into his touch with a soft smile.

Turning away from the sight, Becca saw Reuben and Ruth sitting with their linked hands resting on the bulk of their unborn child. Ruth leaned against her husband's shoulder.

A hand on Becca's shoulder made her start in surprise.

"Come, I will take my own precious burden up to bed as well." Cutter slipped knowing hands beneath his daughter and lifted her limp form to his shoulder. She muttered in her sleep and instantly adjusted herself into a comfortable position against her father's chest. Pressing his lips to his daughter's smooth cheek, Cutter sent his wife another smile before setting off for the loft Becca and Caroline now shared with Ima.

Becca followed him, climbing slowly up the wide-runged ladder, hoping he would quickly settle his daughter in and leave. She had no reason to distrust Cutter, but then, experience had given her little reason to trust any man. She did not want to be alone with him one moment longer than necessary.

"She may snore a little, but a quick nudge will set her quiet if she bothers you." Cutter quickly tucked his daughter into a cotton nightgown and settled her into bed.

"I doubt she will bother me; I sleep hard myself." Becca settled Caroline on the corn-shuck mattress beside Ima. When would he leave?

He smoothed his hand along his daughter's hair before turning to face Becca. "I am sorry we cannot offer more comfortable accommodations to you."

"These are better than I've had in some time. Beggars cannot be choosers." She shrugged stiffly, making sure to keep the bed positioned between them.

He had been nothing but kind to her. However, her caution was instinctive. This man took much sass from his own wife without raising a hand or even his voice, but that did not mean he would not abuse Becca. There was a wild grace in the way he moved, and more than once, as he and Mack talked about the dangers of frontier life, she had seen a latent violence in his eyes. It would be very wise to exhibit caution around such a man.

He gave her a gentle smile. As if he sensed her unease, he moved away from the bed and toward the open hatch. "There is no need to beg. You may have a place here as long as you like, Rebecca Wallace."

She bit down on her lip and flushed guiltily. She should not be afraid. Seeing how his wife and even Ruth, who was once a slave, felt free to tease and argue with the man should have told her all she needed to know. And she should have trusted Mack not to bring her anywhere but a place of safety.

She offered Cutter a tentative smile. "That is very kind of you. You are kind people. I told Mack as much when we talked earlier." She could not keep her bitterness from her voice, remembering the way Mack had spoken to her.

Cutter gave her a quiet look, his smile fading. "I think I owe you an apology for that. He was in a devil of a mood when we returned from scouting, and I fear it is my fault.''

An apology? That made her look up. She could not remember any man ever apologizing to her. Other than Mack, of course. She didn't know what to say. "I don't think you fear much."

"Only my wife's temper, and that was the start of the trouble.'' His lips twisted into a crooked smile.

She returned his smile, trying to hide her awkwardness. "Do not worry yourselves over it. Mack and I had our troubles long before we arrived here.''

"That is unusual for Mack. He normally has quite a way with the ladies.''

She straightened her shoulders, not liking the reminder. "I understand he does, but he says I am nothing like the other women he's known.''

"I believe that is true, but then, Mack has long believed, mistakenly I might add, that women are much alike. I think this lesson has been a long time coming.''

"I am glad he has received some benefit out of our relationship.''

"He has realized more than that. More than you know. More than he is willing to admit.''

"I am certain there is nothing to admit." She paced stiffly around the bed, avoiding the sloping roof. The room was large enough, she need not step too near Cutter.

"I am not so certain." Cutter shook his head and gave her a searching look. "That is why I wanted to speak to you, Becca. To help you understand. Emily and I pushed him into that foul mood. We had words with him about you."

"About me?" She twisted the folds of her skirt in her hands and tried not to worry about the implications. Surely they did not mean to send her away? No. That could not be it; Cutter had already assured her that she could stay here in the safety of Cutright Station, the first place she had ever felt safe—except for in Mack's arms. But she could not afford to think about that now, not when Cutter was still speaking.

"We knew from the first that you are different to Mack than the other women he's known. We can see it in the way he looks at you." Cutter's lips twisted into a wry smile. "I could see it in the way he looked at me when I dared lift you from the horse."

"He is protective of me. He sees it as his duty." She fought to keep her tone level, to not let her voice show how much she hated that fact.

"When you came into my home, you came under *my* protection. I will not let any man abuse you, not even the man who brought you here."

That was one fear she could set at ease. She lifted her eyes to meet his steady gaze. "He has never abused me. I know what abuse is. Mack does not have it in him to treat a woman that way."

"No. But he does have it in him to take advantage of a woman, and I won't have it."

The vehemence in his voice surprised her. She was still unused to people caring about her. It seemed everyone at Cutright's Station cared about her, but the one she most wanted to care. "You have no need to worry about that. Mack cannot even look at me any longer. He cannot bear to be near me." She looked away from his gaze, not wanting this man she barely knew to see the hurt in her eyes.

"That is only a symptom, Becca."

"A symptom of what?"

"The way he feels about you."

Unable to be still under his regard, even in the dim light of a single candle, Becca puttered around the room, needlessly straightening clothing. "He only feels a responsibility for me, nothing more. He has made that quite clear."

She couldn't keep the bitterness from her voice.

Cutter stopped her with a touch to her shoulder. "He is a good man."

"I know that."

"Do you? Do you know that in here?" Cutter laid his hand over his heart. "He is not an easy man to know."

She hesitated to ask, but she needed to know, and there might not be such a chance to ask again. "What haunts him?"

Cutter shook his head. "That is something you will have to ask Mack. It is not my secret to share."

"But he will share nothing with me. That is what he has decided."

"Tomorrow you will have to ask my wife about our courtship. There were many things that I decided, for her good and mine, and Emily decided differently. In the end it was her will that prevailed—to my eternal gratitude."

"Your wife is a strong woman."

"And you are not?"

Unable to answer him, she shifted her gaze from his, unable to bear his searching look.

"Good night, Becca. Do not be too hard on my friend." He stepped down the ladder and turned back to face her before his shoulders descended through the opening. "Mack is a fool about many things, but he would not make the mistake of falling in love with a weak woman."

Becca's tired body demanded rest, but she could not stop her mind from working over the things Cutter had told her. She knew from Emily that Mack and Cutter's friendship went back a long way. Cutter must know Mack well, but could still be mistaken about what lay hidden in his friend's heart.

Yet she remembered, all too well, the way Mack had looked at her tonight. He had refused to sit with his friends, despite Ima's tearful pleading, but he had been unable to keep his eyes off her. Even when she had tried everything to forget his presence, laughing with Tad and singing with Reuben, she had felt his gaze upon her.

More than that, she remembered the way he had looked at her their last night on the trail. The way his hands worshipped her body, the way his lips teased hers. . . .

Stifling a moan with her fist, she turned on the rustling corn-husk mattress, careful not to wake the sleeping baby and child. The Cutrights had been so generous to offer her a home, but how could she stay here, within sight and sound of a man who wanted her so badly and would do nothing but torture himself—and her—in the bargain?

* * *

"You shouldn't be out here. Cutter told you to stay inside the walls today." Mack didn't even look up from the row of corn he was weeding.

She couldn't see a weed in sight, and the ground was so churned he must have been working in this same spot for some time. The sight was some consolation to her for her own sleepless night. It was good to know she was not alone in her suffering. "He did no such thing. He only said I need not work in the fields today."

"You should not be here."

"I thought you hardworking men might welcome a drink of water, but if you'd rather choke on your own bile, then you are welcome to it."

She turned so quickly she bumped the bucket against her knee, sloshing water on her foot. The cold well water felt good against her hot skin, and she had only just walked from the cool shade of the station walls. She couldn't imagine how hot the men felt after working all morning in the field under the hot summer sun. But she doubted the heat was the reason for Mack's prickly temperature.

"Don't be foolish. Now that you are here I might as well have a drink, but don't come back out again."

Turning around to face him, Becca gave Mack a cool look. "I don't think *I* am the one being foolish here."

He flashed her a dark look and drank from the dipper she handed him. After drinking another dipperful, he splashed water on his face, then stooped to pick up his hoe again.

She smiled brightly. "You're welcome."

But Mack was not paying any attention to her sarcasm. Instead, his attention was caught by something in the trees surrounding the field. He lifted his head and moved his hand to pick up the long rifle that was never far from him.

"What's wrong?" She tightened her grip on the water bucket and wished she had thought to bring a gun with her.

"Someone is in the trees," he told Becca in a low voice. "Get behind the walls. Now. Don't run unless you hear shots or strange voices. Walk quickly and pass the word to Reuben and Cutter as you pass them by."

"But—"

"Just go. I cannot protect you out in the open like this. We will both die if you stay. Go!"

CHAPTER 15

"What is it?" Emily asked as Becca carefully shut the small door cut in the station gate.

She leaned against the door, trying to regain control of her trembling legs. "Mack saw someone in the trees." Her fingers ached from clutching the handle of the bucket so tightly. It had taken every ounce of control she could muster to walk back to the gates; she had never wanted to run so badly.

Emily slid an arm around Becca's shoulders to offer comfort, but her expression was all business. "Friend or foe?"

"He doesn't know, but he wasn't taking any chances."

"Then, neither will we." Emily pulled her away from the door. "Can you shoot?"

Becca bit her lip, remembering the horror of the dead Indian's warm blood splattering her arms, but she also remembered the Indian's taunting laughter as he dangled her baby above a blazing fire. And Mack was still out there in the field, vulnerable despite the presence of the other men. She nodded firmly. "Yes. Should I go up in the tower?"

Emily rested her hand on the small mound of her belly. "You best, at least until the men come in. You are the only one of us who can lie flat, and that is the best way to take advantage of the protection of the tower's walls.

"Ruth, you keep watch on the gate and be ready to open it for our men if they make a run for it. I will be watching out the gun port beside it to cover their retreat."

"You will watch over Caroline?" Taking the rifle and powder horn Ruth brought her, Becca looked toward the basket by the cabin door where her baby slept. She wanted to hold her daughter for just one moment, but knew there was no time.

"We will guard her well," Emily promised. "Now go!"

Once upon the tower, Becca lay on her stomach, resting her arms on a pile of sacking, and peered out the gun slit cut into the log wall surrounding the small fortress. Nothing much had changed in the field except the men were now working closer together than before—and farther from the tree line.

The only one of the four men really working was Reuben. Mack, Cutter and Tad still held hoes in their hands, giving the appearance of work; but their eyes kept scanning the trees, and their guns lay beside them to be picked up at the first hint of danger.

Something caught Mack's attention. At his word, all the men picked up their weapons with well-practiced quickness. Becca's breath caught in her throat as she watched two Indians step from the trees, and she caressed the trigger of her rifle.

Suddenly recognizing the pair, she set the gun down with a thud and managed to let out the air in her lungs.

"Don't shoot, Becca!" Emily called up to her. "These are friends. Stay up and keep watch until all are safely inside the walls."

As she watched Big Fist and Otter walk with the men toward the station gates, Becca's heart twisted painfully. Mack was laughing at something the younger warrior had said. At that moment she knew, no matter whether Cutter was right or wrong about where Mack's affections lay, she felt something more for Silas McGee than gratitude and friendship.

Something deeper than was good for her. No. She shook her head. She was not in love with him. This could not be love. She would not let it be love. Whatever this emotion, gratitude and something more, she would force it to stop there.

Long after the gate closed behind the men and all were safely behind the station walls, Becca lay in the tower, struggling to make sense of her newfound knowledge. This was the worst thing that could have happened. Just when she was finally free of men, when she had finally found a safe place, she had allowed herself to become vulnerable. It was not a happy thought.

Especially knowing there was no future in such

feelings. Even if Cutter was right and Mack cared for her, it would not be enough to overcome the dark secrets that tortured his soul. Even if she was right, and her feelings for Mack were more than she was willing to admit, it would not be enough to overcome the pain of her past. The only thing that was certain in her mind was that acting on her feelings for Mack would be a grave mistake. And yet she couldn't help wondering what it would be like, to love and be loved.

If she had not come here, she would not even know what she was missing, and she still didn't—not really. Watching the two married couples at Cutright's Station had shown her there was something she was missing in life, but she was convinced she could make do without it. She would just have to find a way to live with her own secret. She had lived with pain and fear. She could live without love.

When she emerged from the shadows of the kitchen, the others were gathered around their visitors in the station yard. Surprised to see Emily and Tad talking in the Indians' guttural language, Becca watched, stunned, as Emily kissed the younger brave's cheek and then bustled toward the kitchen.

She waved Becca to follow her inside. "Come. We have work to do. They have been doing much spying on our behalf, and the least we can do is make sure to feed them well before we send them back out into danger."

"You can talk to them?" Becca said stupidly as she followed Emily and Ruth into the kitchen.

Emily slid her a teasing look. "Of course, Otter is my brother."

Becca could tell the other woman was making fun of her, but she did not understand. "But you are white."

"His parents adopted me when I lived with the Shawnee for a time before my marriage."

"You lived with the savages?"

Frowning slightly, Emily set down the bowl of corn she had been grinding and turned to face Becca. "I know you have suffered greatly at the hands of some red men. One group killed your husband, and another pair would have killed you and Caroline if you hadn't fought back. But I want you to think about what you just said. Mack told us you spent two days with Big Fist and Otter on your journey here. Are they really savages?"

Becca looked away from her new friend and shook her head, unable to speak in her embarrassment.

Emily set her hands on her hips. "Of course not. They are men, nothing more. There are good white men and bad white men. The same is true of red men. These are good men; otherwise my man and yours would not call them friends. Now, go see if any of my hens are laying, will you? I'm going to try to make a cake. Big Fist has a sweet tooth."

The men continued to talk as they ate, tension radiating from all except Otter, who laughed and teased Ima by pulling her braids. The little girl chattered back at him in his own language. Her obvious teasing earned a round of jeering laughter directed at Otter from the adults who understood.

Unable to stand not knowing the cause of the tension, Becca laid a hand on Tad's arm to draw his attention. For some reason Cutter's teenage son did not generate the fear that most men caused in her. It might have been his quiet demeanor, the gentle way he treated his younger sister, or the simple fact he was not yet fully a man.

"What are they saying?" she whispered in the boy's ear.

"There are war parties all over the territory." He shifted in his seat in obvious discomfort. "Yours was not the only cabin burned, but so far no one else has been killed. The others were warned in time."

"Mack would have been in time for us, too. It is my fault he failed in that mission."

Tad gave her a curious glance, but did not press her for an explanation. She was surprised Mack had not told his friends about her husband, or maybe she shouldn't be surprised. Mack hadn't spent time talking about much of anything to anyone of late. The only time he would say more than one sentence was when Ima asked him a question or when he and Cutter needed to talk about the safety of the station.

Suddenly, Mack smacked the table with his fist, making the wooden platters on it clatter and interrupting the conversation with their guests. Startled by the noise and his sharp tone, Caroline started crying. Big Fist moved to the cradle before Becca could reach her baby. He lifted the child, murmuring soft words.

Becca reached for her daughter, knowing Big Fist would not hurt the child, but still not comfortable with the sight of her baby in Indian hands. Caroline stopped crying, staring with wide eyes at the big warrior. She reached for his beaded braids and gave them a strong tug. Big Fist laughed, running a gentle hand over the baby's downy red curls, and handed the child to Becca with a stream of words she could not understand.

Emily laughed before translating. "He says your daughter has as much spirit and strength as her mother. He says Mack is lucky with such a wife and child." She gave Mack a speculative look. "Now, what does he mean by that, I wonder?"

"I had to say something when they found me traveling with a woman and child." Mack glared at Cutter as if daring him to say something. "But since it is not true, I do not see what is stopping me from going out with this pair to see what is moving about."

"They may not be your woman and child, but they are still your responsibility, or have you forgotten that?"

Cutter carefully filled his pipe with tobacco and handed the pouch to Big Fist, who filled a pipe he pulled from the pouch he wore about his waist. Cutter lit the pipes with a twig he started from the kitchen fire and puffed calmly as he watched Mack.

Glaring at his friend for a long moment, Mack turned on his heel and slammed out of the kitchen without answering.

"He will be back," Cutter said to Becca. "Do not worry."

"That is what I am worried about." Looking at the empty door, Becca held her daughter against her aching heart. Would it be easier to come to terms with herself if she never saw Mack again?

After the Indians left the next morning, the men prepared to go out to the fields again, and Becca's offer to go with them was forcefully turned down. They did allow her to work in the kitchen garden just outside the walls within steps of the gate.

"And you will keep a gun beside you at all times," Cutter repeated for the third time. He gave the tree line a nervous glance, obviously having second thoughts about letting Becca out from the protection of the walls.

"I understand. I have no wish to put myself in danger again. I won't stray far from the walls."

"See that you don't," Mack snapped as he stalked past them, a hoe on one shoulder and a rifle on the other.

Those had been the only words he directed at Becca all day. She stared after him, not wanting to think about the sharp pain in her heart his anger caused.

"Don't mind him, he is only irritable because he must work in the field again." Emily smiled at Becca as she slipped her arm through her husband's. "He thinks farming is beneath his skills. I told him that if he is going to stand watch, he might as well hoe corn while he is at it. Maybe he will be in better humor if he works some of that frustration out on the weeds."

"Maybe we should move to the fort for the summer until things settle down." Cutter frowned as he scanned the tree line again. "At least you, Ruth, Becca and the children can go, while Reuben and I take care of things here."

"Ruth is determined her baby will be born in her home, and that is what I want as well. More important than that, neither of us is willing to be separated from our men." She gave his arm a reassuring pat. "Do not worry overmuch about things, my love. We are safe enough here with the number of guns we have, and you heard what Big Fist and Otter said. The target will most likely be Boonesborough. This number of braves have not traveled here to attack a small station like ours."

"You are certain you would not feel safer in Boonesborough?" Cutter circled his wife's waist and pulled her close so he could study her face.

Becca turned away, her gaze falling on Mack as he worked the hoe along a row of corn. Whichever direction she looked, there was cause for discomfort. Watching the loving couple beside her hurt, but watching Mack deliberately turn so he did not have to see her was even more painful.

If only she could understand him. If only she knew what tormented him so. If only she didn't care.

The day passed quietly with no sign of Indians—friendly or unfriendly. Watching Ruth rub her lower back and stretch after serving their evening meal, Becca firmly sent her to rest and took it upon herself to clean the kitchen and scrub dishes.

She dismissed Ruth's thanks with a wave of her hand, answering truthfully that she would rather be alone for a time. She needed that time to come to terms with her newly discovered feelings for Mack and to make plans for her future. She had never really believed that she would have the opportunity to plan a future that did not include her abusive husband, and now it was time to make some choices.

The Cutrights had made it plain that she could stay with them. They meant her to stay as a welcome guest, but Becca was not sure she would ever feel more than a servant here, and she wanted more for her daughter than that. And there was Mack. Staying with the Cutrights would mean seeing him often. She was not sure that would be a good idea—for either of them.

"You do not need to do this alone." Emily touched Becca's shoulder.

Startled out of her reverie, Becca flinched away instinctively from a strange touch.

Turning, she saw the pensive look on Emily's face.

"I was dreaming," Becca said defensively, and set to scrubbing the bowl in her hands. "I will do better. I am almost finished here."

"You have nothing to apologize for. I simply said you do not have to do this alone. You are a guest, not a servant."

"I must do my part." She scrubbed harder.

"You have done your part and then some." Emily smiled at her. "You best take care that I do not take advantage. I am not known for my love of house-wifery."

"You have been so kind, I want to repay you."

"Becca, kindness is meant to be just that. It is not a debt. There is no question of repayment. There will come a time when your kindness can be shared with someone else in need.''

Becca bent her head over her task, unable to meet Emily's gaze.

"I think this is clean by now," Emily said quietly and lifted the wooden bowl from Becca's hands. "What were you thinking about with such a fierce expression?"

"The future." Caught off guard, Becca answered without thinking. Biting down on her lip, she gave Emily a worried glance.

Emily patted her arm reassuringly. "There is no need to worry. Cutter and Mack will make sure we are safe."

"I know. I have good reason to believe in Mack's ability to protect me." Becca looked down at her hands, surprised to see them twisted together.

"It is not the danger that has you worried, is it?" Emily stowed the bowl away and turned back to study Becca. "It is Mack. He is but a man, Becca, and all men are fools at least some of the time."

"I cannot imagine Cutter being a fool."

"He's been foolish enough a time or two. It was Mack who helped Cutter see reason when he loved me and would have none of it. Cutter would return the favor, if you wished it."

"I do not." Surprised by her vehemence, Becca shifted away from the table to put away the clean dishes and neaten the leftover food.

"What do you wish?"

"I wish for peace. That is all I ask of Mack, but he cannot even give me that."

Feeling the other woman's gaze on her, Becca took longer than necessary to bank the kitchen fire for the night.

"Becca!"

She straightened her shoulders, worrying about the spark of anger in Emily's voice.

"Who has hurt you? Was it Mack?"

"No. He could not; he would not. No." Stumbling over her answer, Becca finally pressed her lips together to stop the words.

The light of anger fading from her eyes, Emily took Becca's hand in hers and pulled her down on the bench beside the table. "You are right. He would not. I should have known that of him, but it makes me so angry the way some men treat women. It was a man, was it not?"

"Yes." The question followed Emily's rapid-fire commentary so naturally, Becca was left with no defenses.

"Your husband."

It was not a question, but Becca answered anyway. This was one secret she did not want to keep. "Yes."

"Did you love him?"

"No. I had no choice but to marry him, and I thought he was the better choice. My stepfather was a brutal man. Hugh was a better choice, but not by much."

"And now you are glad he is dead?" Emily asked softly.

Ashamed, Becca turned her face away. She was glad and guilty, too. "It is my fault he is dead."

"Why? Did you wish him dead?" Emily said briskly.

"If he is dead by your very hand, then he has no one but himself to blame."

"Hugh never got to hear Mack's warning because he was protecting me. I'd run away."

"Good for you. You may be a match for Mack yet!"

"No! That cannot be. Do not even think it."

Emily gave her a long look. "Now I know what you are afraid of."

CHAPTER 16

After climbing to the tower, Mack leaned back on his elbows, watching the forest take shape in the pre-dawn light. Birds sang and chattered as they prepared for the day while the rest of nature was silent. He was alone in the world, and that was the way he wanted it.

He cleared his mind of everything but the soft touch of the morning breeze across his face that carried the moist scent of dew. Closing his eyes, he listened to the sad call of a mourning dove and felt the tension ease from him. This was the way life was meant to be. No complications. No distractions. No troubles.

The sweet scent of roses warned him he was not going to have his way for long. Sitting up, he did not look toward the open hatch, knowing what was to come. His stomach tightened.

"Good morning, Mack," she said softly as she

climbed the ladder to join him. She sat beside him, not touching him, but close enough that he could feel the warmth of her body and remember how it felt to hold her.

He nodded at her, barely turning his head to acknowledge her presence. She did not take the hint.

She sighed deeply. "I must speak with you, Mack."

"Then speak." He did not really want to hear what she had to say, not when it would force him to lie to her again. He did not like lying, and especially not to Becca.

He would listen. He would lie. But he would not look at her. He had already learned he could not look her in the eye and watch those big green eyes fill with tears because he had hurt her.

He could not do that.

She paused for a moment as if waiting for him to say something more. "What do you see when you look at me?"

Despite his intent, he could not help turning to look at her. This was not what he had thought she would say. He studied her from her sleep-tousled curls to the way her hands lay folded and still in her lap. As always she looked beautiful. As always he desired her. But he could not puzzle out what she wanted from him.

He answered her with caution. "A woman." What did she expect him to say?

"But what kind of woman?" She shifted her seat to meet his eyes, a wrinkle of concentration creased her forehead. "I have never thought of myself in such simple terms before. Always I have belonged to someone else. I've been someone's daughter or someone's wife. Now I can simply belong to myself, but where does that leave me?"

Was she asking him to declare himself? No. He had already made himself clear. She knew he would not marry her. Looking at her worried expression, he could only suppose she was concerned about her future. Weren't they all.

"Free. It leaves you free." How he envied her that.

"Free," she repeated to herself as if testing the word and the sensation. "But what will I do with my freedom?"

"That is the beauty of it, Becca. Only you can decide. If I decide for you, then you are not free."

"I will have to think on that," she said softly, drawing her legs up against her chest and resting her chin on her knees. "I know I've truly been free for more than two weeks now, but our journey here was so uncertain that I never dared think about the future. But now I feel safe. Safe enough to dare think about the future.

"It seems that is all I have been thinking about of late. Thinking kept me from sleeping well. Have you been doing some thinking as well? Is that why you are up with the birds and spend as little time in the company of others as you can?"

"I slept just fine," he answered brusquely, knowing it for a lie. "I am up early by choice. I like to see the sunrise when I can. You never know when you will not see another."

The sky was brightening in the east. Sunrise was not far away. He concentrated on the sky, but it did not help. He was all too aware of the woman beside him. His position allowed him to study her at will, her profile outlined against the lightening horizon.

Turning quickly, she touched his arm with a gesture so light and quick he might have imagined it. "I am sorry, Mack." Her voice caught on the words.

He almost reached out to comfort her, but he knew it would be a mistake to touch her. "For what are you sorry?"

"For doing this to you."

He narrowed his eyes at her. "What exactly do you think you have done?"

She worried her lower lip between her teeth. If only she knew what that gesture did to the pit of his stomach. "I have made you bitter and withdrawn. You were not this way when we met. I am sorry that knowing me has changed you like this."

He could not let her know the depth of his weakness. "You are not the center of the world, Becca. You have not changed me."

She reached toward him again, but after meeting his angry gaze, she let her hand fall to her lap without touching him. "Then, what has?"

"Why do you care? I brought you to safety, and I stay here, against my wishes, to keep you safe. What more do you want from me?"

"Can we not be friends?"

"I cannot be friends with a woman." Another lie. It was only this woman he could not have as a friend.

"You are friends with Emily."

"That is different. I am friends with her husband. She is an extension of Cutter."

"Do not let her hear you say that." She gave him a tentative smile.

"I am wiser than that." His lips curved slightly at the thought of Emily's fury, but the motion felt awkward and stiff. He couldn't remember the last time he had smiled.

"But not wise enough to share your burdens with the people who care about you."

"Do not care about me, Becca," he warned. "There is nothing but trouble there."

"You told me I was free to do as I wish." She lifted her chin to a stubborn angle. "That means I can care about you. I do not have to do as you tell me. We've already established you have no hold on me."

"Except for one thing. I am responsible for your safety, and it is not safe to care about me. That is a proven fact."

"How was it proven?"

"You do not need to know."

"Mack, do not push me away. I can be a very stubborn woman." She shifted so she knelt beside him.

She was too close. He turned his head to find something, anything, to fix his concentration on. "You cannot be more stubborn than a Scotsman. Do not even try it."

She touched his cheek so he would look at her. Her caress burned him as she met his gaze straight on. "Not even a Scotsman can match a Scotswoman for stubbornness."

She leaned in and kissed him.

The need to return her kiss, to hold her, was stronger than his ability to remember the reasons why he shouldn't. He groaned against her mouth and pulled her onto his lap. The soft fullness of her breasts pressed against his chest. The round curves of her bottom teased his aching manhood.

But it was only a kiss. It was wrong to touch her. It was wrong to hold her. But it was only a kiss.

A kiss that deepened as her mouth opened beneath his assault. A kiss that brought his blood to a boil. A kiss that narrowed the world so his senses were aware only of her—the slick heat of her mouth, the sweet taste of her breath, the soft feel of her skin.

When he came back to his senses, Mack found his hands unfastening her bodice. He forced them down to his sides.

Becca did not move from his lap. She smiled and traced his lower lip with her finger. "That was nice. I think I will like having the freedom to choose. I wonder what I will choose next?"

He did not dare to wonder. Already his blood had pooled to his groin, and he was finding it difficult to concentrate on anything but the simple fact he wanted the woman leaning against him to nibble on his earlobe.

"Becca!" He forced himself to remember she was a new-made widow. He forced himself to remember he was responsible for her safety. He forced himself to remember. . . .

She wiggled her hips, and he couldn't remember his name until she whispered it against his mouth. "Mack, why aren't you holding me?"

He couldn't remember any of the reasons why he shouldn't, so he pulled her tight against him. When her tongue teased the line of his lips, he teased her back with his tongue and lost all track of time.

"We missed the sunrise," Becca said softly, tracing his jaw with her hand.

Looking over her shoulder, Mack saw she was right. He also saw some movement along the edge of the forest. Even as he watched, a horse and rider broke through the brush bordering the crops. He rode straight across the corn field, heedless of the waving green plants, beating his tattered hat against his horse's sweat-darkened flank.

Mack tightened his arms around Becca. The rider was a white man and his gun was strapped to his saddle, so he was obviously no immediate threat. But Mack knew the man brought danger with him.

He didn't want to let Becca go, but knew his arms offered her no protection at all. He set her aside. "We must go down."

" 'Ware the station!" the rider shouted as he made for the station gates, trampling through the garden where Becca had pulled weeds only yesterday.

Tad must have recognized the rider's voice, because he ran to fling open the gate before Mack and Becca could even take to the ladder.

The man—no, it was a boy Mack saw now that he was closer—rode right into the station yard and started shouting before he even dismounted. "Indians struck a station a day's ride south of here. They carried off two boys who didn't make it inside the walls in time."

Becca went pale and wobbled as she tried to stand. Mack put an arm around her to steady her and knew it would be the last time he would touch her. He could not risk her again.

Out of breath, the boy slid from his horse and waited for the station's residents to gather around him. He obviously only wanted to share his news once. Mack could not blame him.

When Mack and Becca joined the others in the yard, Cutter nodded at the boy to deliver his message.

"They're going after the raiders." Setting his face into a hard expression that ill matched his freckles and cowlick, the boy drew himself to his full height. "Men from Boonesborough, Lexington, Harrod's and Bryan's Station are joining up to go after them. Colonel Boone's come in to lead 'em, but it will leave the settlements with scant protection. He's telling folks to go into one of the bigger forts for safety."

Hearing Becca's soft gasp at his side, Mack ground his teeth together. He wanted to hold her and comfort her, but it was not to be. The only thing he could do was protect her, and he couldn't do that if he touched her. That would be her doom.

"We won't leave our home," Emily said firmly, glaring at her husband before he could commit them to moving to Boonesborough.

"We will discuss that when we fully understand the situation." Cutter's quiet voice was filled with determination to match his wife's. "How many in the war party?"

"Upwards of sixty or seventy, we was told by a man who managed to get away without being noticed." The boy took a dipper of water that Tad offered him and drank deeply. "They was heading north with the fellers they took, but that don't mean they won't double back.''

"Or that they are the only war party on the move," Mack said grimly, stroking the stock of his long rifle. "Taking our women and children from the safety of this station to Boonesborough could mean leading them straight into the arms of another war party."

"I didn't see nothing on my way here, but that don't mean there's nothing out there," the boy agreed. "I've got to get going. There's more folks that need to hear my news. You folks do what you think best."

Tad watered the horse and rubbed it down while Emily fed the messenger a quick meal. They scarcely closed the gates behind him before Emily whirled on her husband with anger glinting in her eyes. "I will not be driven from my home, so don't even think it Stephen Cutright."

"We cannot hold out against a war party that large, and you know it, Emily. Be reasonable."

"Mack made an important point. We will be vulnerable on the trail, and even if we make it safely to Boonesborough, we have no way to know we would be any safer."

"Boonesborough's walls are higher and stronger, and there are more men to defend them. You will be safer in Boonesborough."

"I am willing to take the risk to defend my home. We've built this station with our hands. We've loved here. Our daughter was born here." Emily's voice caught, and she drew in a ragged breath. "I will not abandon it."

Mack's heart ached for her. Normally, he would support her argument. Normally, he would be willing to lay down his life to protect his friends and their home. But now there was Becca. He could not put himself at risk, not when she still needed him.

Concentrating on his wife, Cutter stroked her cheek. "We can build a new home; but I cannot replace you, Emily, and I could not bear to lose you. Would you destroy me to have your way?"

"Cutter . . ." She went into his arms.

The sight tore at Mack's heart. Only moments before he had held a woman that he . . . that he must protect.

"What do you think, Mack?" Cutter looked over his wife's head to meet his friend's gaze.

Mack glanced quickly at Becca standing beside him, cradling Caroline in her arms. He remembered her fierce determination to survive and to protect her daughter. She would stand shoulder-to-shoulder with him on any battlefield he chose, but he could not risk her either. He had not brought her to Cutright's Station to die.

"You have enough horses to mount everyone. I say we make a run for it, but we better move fast. Tad and I can move out ahead and scout out any danger. You and Reuben should stay with the women for protection. Becca and Emily are both fair shots."

Ruth moaned softly and sagged against her husband as she scooped her hands under the huge mound of her belly as if to cradle her unborn child.

Emily and Becca hurried to her. Mack watched in

fascination as Ruth's belly seemed to ripple and move beneath her dress.

"Cutter! We can't leave now." Emily gave Ruth a worried glance.

"This baby won't be born yet. I can ride for the fort. I won't hold you back." Ruth grunted in pain as another contraction seized her. "I won't put y'all in danger."

Cutter did not hesitate. "Reuben, take your wife back to bed. We will face whatever comes here in our home. My wife was right the first time. We cannot leave our home. Do not worry, Ruth. We will protect you and your baby."

Mack waited until Reuben carried Ruth from the station yard before rounding on Cutter. "We cannot afford to wait for that baby to be born. We either make for the fort or we stay here to die."

Becca set down the pail of water she had just drawn from the well and stepped between the glaring men. "There will be no dying today. Now do what you must to guard us, but do not interfere, Silas McGee. This is woman's work. We will welcome a new life, and that is the way it should be. And it is nothing you know about."

CHAPTER 17

Mack caught Becca's arm before she could step away from him. "Do you not understand the danger?"

"Go on to Boonesborough, then, if you are afraid." She scowled at him and pulled her arm free.

He shouldn't touch her, he knew, but he was willing to risk anything to protect her. He was willing to risk anything for her. Wrapping his arms around her, he pulled her against him. She trembled in his embrace, but her eyes blazed in anger. "Let me go!"

"You are right. I am afraid, but not for myself." He kissed her fiercely, promising himself it was for the last time. He did not want to think about the way it felt to hold her, the way it touched off more than passion. He forced himself to concentrate on the need to protect her. "I am afraid for you. I am afraid for Caroline. I am afraid for both of you."

Her expression softened, and she stopped struggling to free herself. She reached up to touch his face gently. "We are all afraid, Mack, but all we can do is try our best not to let that fear rule our lives. I trust you to protect me."

He froze, his heart in his throat. That was not what he wanted to hear. "Don't you see! I am afraid I cannot. This place was not built to withstand an attack like we may face. Seventy warriors! We may not even have enough ammunition to fight a prolonged battle against so many."

She smiled softly as she stroked his cheek. "Mack, I must put my safety in your hands and trust that will be enough. I cannot think about it now. Ruth needs me."

"You won't leave, then?" He released his hold. He didn't want to feel her warmth any longer, not when he feared her body would soon grow cold from death. His heart ached at the thought. "You won't even try to save yourself?"

She shook her head as she stepped back from his embrace. "I cannot. Don't you see? I am needed here. I am wanted here. I've never known that before. It is a wonderful feeling."

She disappeared into the cabin before he could tell her that he wanted her, that he needed her. He should have been relieved that he had not made that mistake. He should have been, but he was not. All he knew was how wrong she was to trust him and how wrong she was about being needed and wanted.

It was a terrible feeling.

* * *

Becca dabbed cool water on Ruth's face as the black woman lay back and panted.

"I never knew this was so hard!" Ruth scowled at Emily, who knelt at the foot of the bed. "You did not have it so hard. You squirted that Ima-girl out so fast I could barely catch her!"

Emily laughed and reached up to squeeze Ruth's hand. "It was hardly that easy, and you should know it is different for every woman, and for every baby, I hear." She rubbed her hand across the gentle swell of her belly. "I may not have such an easy time of it this time around."

Ruth screamed and grimaced as another contraction took hold. Closing her eyes, she gripped Becca's hand so tightly she feared her bones would shatter.

Becca did not begrudge her new friend the pain. She remembered all too well how it felt to labor to give birth. She remembered the pain and the fear. Wiping sweat from the other woman's forehead, Becca knew she could understand Ruth's pain and fear, but she wondered if she would ever be able to understand Ruth's joy and anticipation.

When Ruth was not cursing the pain, she was eagerly speculating about her baby.

Becca loved her daughter, but the child had meant another tie to Hugh Wallace, another weapon he could use against her, another way to make her vulnerable. She had feared for her child from the moment of her birth. Ruth would never have that fear. She was loved, and her child would be loved. Becca couldn't help but wonder what it would be like to know so much love.

Just remembering the feel of Mack's arms around her made her lips curve into a smile, but such thoughts were dangerous. There would be no future with him. Mack had told her she was free to choose any future she wanted, but she knew he meant any future but one with him. She was beginning to fear, fear very much, that was exactly the future she most wanted.

Ruth moaned and drew Becca back to the moment.

Ruth's belly rippled as the baby moved inside, and Emily lay her hand on the huge mound, giving Ruth a reassuring smile. "Your baby is doing just fine, Ruth. Soon you will be able to hold him in your arms, and then you will know it is all worth while."

"I want my baby to be a girl!" Ruth insisted, leaning back again to rest. "I've had enough of men for a while."

"That's what you think now, but you'll forget that soon enough. You remember I told Cutter he wouldn't sleep in my bed for years after Ima was born." Emily massaged the mound of Ruth's belly.

"You took him back before the month was out if'n I remember right." Ruth laughed before another contraction caused her to grimace.

Emily's self-satisfied smile was all the answer needed. Becca worried her lip between her teeth, wondering what it would be like to love a man that much, to want a man that much. She was willing to

admit she wanted Mack, but there was some safety in
desiring a man who would always push her away.

"Reuben won't be that lucky." Ruth bit off her
sentence and twisted in the bed, fighting through
another contraction.

Ruth turned her head away, but not before Becca
caught sight of the tears in her eyes. Stroking Ruth's
hair, Becca leaned in when the contraction subsided
to whisper softly to her. "You will be fine. Your baby
will be born healthy, and you will watch her grow.
All this will be forgotten."

Ruth shifted in a futile attempt to find a comfortable position. "I wish she would hurry up and be
born already. We could still make it to the fort."

"We're not going anywhere today, even if that baby
is born this minute." Emily scowled at Ruth, even as
her hands gently stroked the other woman's heaving
belly. "You both will need your rest, and I'm not
going to risk something happening to either of you
just because my husband worries overmuch."

"I am afraid," Ruth whispered.

"There is no need to be afraid." Becca wiped
Ruth's face with a cloth dipped in cool well water.
"Mack, Cutter and Reuben will see that nothing hap-
pens to us."

"Becca is right. You know Reuben loves you and
this baby so much he could kill a whole tribe of
Indians with his bare hands if he thought they might
harm a hair on your head." Emily straightened the
pillows behind Ruth's back to settle her in a more
upright position.

Ruth did not look reassured. "I have a bad feeling. Something bad gonna happen. I jest know it."

"The Indians won't attack. Big Fist and Otter have seen no sign anywhere near us. We're safe enough here and maybe safer than at Boonesborough." Emily took Ruth's hand in hers as another contraction swept over her friend.

When she was able to lie still again, Ruth gasped for breath. "I'm afraid I won't live through this. If'n the injuns don't get me, then I'll die here in this bed anyway. I'm sore afraid."

"That is just the pain and tiredness taking over." Becca patted Ruth's arm reassuringly. "Nothing bad is going to happen to you. Emily and I won't let it, and you know no one dares defy Emily, not even Cutter!"

"I'm not that fearsome!" Emily protested, frowning horribly at Becca.

Ruth gave a weak laugh.

"You are and more, and well you know it." Encouraged by Ruth's faint smile, Becca continued her teasing.

"Emily was never frightened." Ruth fought through another contraction before she could speak again. "She was mad and yelled some terrible things at Cutter, but she was never scared."

"I was too scared," Emily snapped. "You know how much being scared makes me mad!"

Ruth smiled at that, but her lips quickly twisted into a grimace as she braced herself for another contraction. When it was over she lay panting, clinging to Becca's hand.

Becca could remember how it felt to be afraid.

"I was scared to death," she said softly. "I thought I was going to die; but you can see I didn't, and Caroline is fine and healthy. I can promise you that it was all worth it, just for her. I would do it all over again without a thought."

"You were scared?" Ruth turned her head to study Becca closely, a flicker of hope in her dark eyes.

"Terrified," Becca assured her. "I was all alone with no women and no one to tell me what to expect. At least you watched Ima be born, so you know what to expect. And Emily and I are here to help you. You aren't alone."

"You were alone with only your husband for help?" Emily shook her head in amazement. "No wonder you were scared. Men are worse than useless at a time like this."

"No. My husband was not there. I was truly alone." Becca looked away. She didn't want to think about that. Hugh was dead and gone now, but she wasn't sure the memories ever would be.

Ruth closed her eyes as another contraction took hold. Emily moved to stand at the foot of the bed. Catching her lip between her teeth, Emily frowned down at Ruth, but when the black woman opened her eyes, her friend gave her a reassuring smile. "I am sure it won't be long now."

"I feel as if I'm lying in a puddle," Ruth said weakly, trying to shift her hips. "Did I wet myself?"

"Nothing so embarrassing as that. Just the fluid that cushioned your baby while he—sorry she—grew. Now she doesn't need it any longer." Emily bustled to the chest in the corner and took out fresh linen. "This is normal, so lie back and rest yourself. Becca and I will quickly clean this mess up."

In no time, Becca and Emily changed the bedding. Emily efficiently bundled the used sheets into a basket in the corner, but not before Becca saw the blood stains soaking through the outer layer. She understood the lines of worry on the other woman's forehead better now. She knew Ruth was having a hard time of it, but she suspected Emily was more worried than she wanted to let on.

"I will get some more water." Becca lifted the empty bucket and carried it to the door. She needed to escape the stifling cabin, if only for a moment, and she had an overwhelming need to hold her daughter. For all her reassuring words to Ruth, Becca couldn't help absorbing some of the other woman's fear.

She barely stepped into the station yard before she was surrounded by men.

"My Ruth, is she . . ." Reuben gripped her arm painfully.

Wincing away from his touch, Becca gave him a reassuring smile and tried not to think about the blood and the fact Ruth's labor was not progressing quickly enough to suit either Emily or Becca. "She is not happy with you right now because she needs someone to blame for the pain, but she is doing well."

Cutter slapped Reuben on the back and took the bucket from Becca. "That is a good sign. A woman who still has the strength to blame her husband for loving her should be strong enough to deliver his child safely. You will see, soon you will be kissing Ruth and holding your child."

Cutter led Reuben away to fill the bucket, leaving Becca alone with Mack. He took her hand and led her to the bench positioned beside the basket where Caroline slept. She didn't lift the sleeping baby into her arms, not wanting to disturb the infant's rest. Instead, she contented herself with cupping her hand around her child's head and watching the rise and fall of her tiny chest.

"You look tired." Mack tucked a loose strand of hair behind her ear. "You should not push yourself so hard."

Becca resisted the impulse to lean against him. If he pushed her away—no, when he pushed her away— it would break her heart, and she didn't have the strength to face it. "I have no choice. Ruth is laboring hard. She cannot be left alone."

Mack watched Cutter and Reuben cross from the well. "Will it be much longer before the baby is born?"

Becca caught her lip between her teeth. "I hope not."

"It is not going well?"

"She is tiring and losing more blood than she should. I do not know how much longer she can go on. I fear if the baby is not born soon, it may be too late." Becca rolled her shoulders in a vain effort to ease their ache.

"It may be too late for all of us. We would be at Boonesborough by now."

"There is no certainty we would be safer there or that we would have arrived at all."

Mack stroked the barrel of his rifle. "I would rather have gambled on that safety."

"I must go back to Ruth." Becca stood. She did not have the energy to argue with him, not when she was needed. "Emily should get some rest."

He caught her hand before she could take a step toward the cabin. "I will do my best to keep you safe."

"I know you will." Looking into his eyes, she could tell he did not believe his words or hers. She wondered once again what was in his past to make him believe only in the bleakest of possibilities.

Ruth's baby was born in the gray hour just before dawn. Emily had slept fitfully on a pallet beside the bed, lying down only when Becca threatened to bring Cutter in to carry her away entirely if she did not rest, but she wakened when Becca called for her. The baby slithered out in a rush of fluid and blood and started screaming before Becca could finish wiping her face.

Ruth was so weak she could hold her baby for only a moment and seemed to fade in and out of awareness. She barely noticed when Emily took the baby to clean her, and did not help lift her arms and legs when Becca bathed her. Even Reuben's joyful examination of his child and tender affection toward his wife barely brought Ruth back to consciousness.

Emily assured the new father that Ruth was just tired and that she would return to normal when she was well rested, but after shutting the cabin door behind him, Emily gave Becca a worried look. "She would not even nurse."

"We can hold the baby to her breast ourselves and see if that will work." Becca shifted the baby to her shoulder, but the newborn girl squawked in protest. Becca felt her breasts tighten in instinctive response to the sound. She was full and ready for Caroline's morning feeding. "This is one hungry baby."

They tried repeatedly to settle Ruth's baby at her breast, but the baby would have none of it. Becca suspected they were not helping matters because the baby could not find a natural position without her mother's help.

Emily cradled the baby and tried to hush her cries, but the newborn's enraged cries only increased in pitch. Ruth did not even waken.

Casting another worried look at Ruth, Becca settled into the rocking chair beside the cold fireplace and lifted her arms to Emily. "Give her to me. I will satisfy her hunger for now. Maybe Ruth will be able to nurse her when she becomes hungry again."

"Are you certain?"

Becca smiled. "I have milk enough for two, and if Caroline does not get her fill, she is old enough to have bread or rice soaked in milk."

"No, that is not what I meant." Emily stroked her finger down the baby's soft cheek as she gave Becca a measured look. "Ruth and Reuben are like family to us, but some white women might not feel the same."

Becca met her gaze dead on. "Ruth has been nothing but kind to me. It would be a poor way to repay her kindness if I let her baby go hungry when I had the means to ease her."

Becca fed both babies, changed them into dry swaddling, and laid them together in the wooden cradle Reuben had built for his child. They would not be able to share a bed for long—Caroline seemed to grow bigger every day—but for now there was room enough for them both.

Something thudded against the cabin wall, the outer wall that was actually part of the palisade wall. She puzzled over the sound, her mind too tired to think straight, when she heard Cutter shout outside. Before she could do more than take a step toward the door to investigate, she heard a chilling cry break through the still, dawn air. Freezing in disbelief and fear, something else caught her attention—the scent of smoke.

She ran for the door, snatching up the water bucket as she went.

"They're trying to burn us out!" Tad shouted to her as she burst through the door.

She quickly scanned the station's building—the barn, kitchen and Emily and Cutter's home positioned in each of the other three corners—but could see no sign of smoke. Turning, she saw flames licking at the roof of the cabin she had just left.

CHAPTER 18

Becca leaned against the rough wall of the kitchen cabin and strained her ears to catch a sound from outside the stockade. There was nothing.

"Do you see anything?" she asked Mack as she fingered the bag of powder that hung around her neck so it would be at hand when she needed it. So far there had been no further attack, but she expected that to change at any moment. This time she would be ready to defend those important to her.

"No." He moved away from the loophole to give her a reassuring smile. "There is nothing in sight any larger than a pair of ground squirrels feasting on the green corn that was trampled by our visitors."

She was not reassured. Maybe because he could not quite mask the worry in his eyes. Maybe because she could sense the cloud of fear that hung over the station. Maybe because she could still smell the acrid stench of burning pitch.

"Why won't they show themselves?" Becca hefted the long rifle leaning against the wall beside her, but Mack took it from her before she could check to see if it was loaded. She didn't protest because she knew it was loaded. She had checked it only moments before. She merely needed something to do, some action to stop her from feeling so helpless.

"There is your answer." He set the rifle back in place. "They do not want to risk being shot."

"How many are out there?"

"I don't know." Mack set his eye to another loophole again and scanned the surrounding land. "I don't think many. That is why they are so quiet now; they are waiting for dark to attack again."

"Just a few? Then, there is no question we can drive them off?"

"There is always a question, Becca. You should know that." He shifted position to look out the other loophole. "However, Cutter has built a stout station, and with us to watch these two walls, Cutter and Emily to watch the opposite corner, and Tad positioned above, we can hold off many times our number."

"But when it gets dark, they can creep right up to the walls, and we would not see them." Becca shuddered. "They could set us afire again."

She tried not to think about the horrifying moment when she saw the roof of the cabin where her child slept ablaze. Tad had beat the flames out with a broom before she could do more than scream Caroline's name, but it still turned her legs to jelly just to think of it. She reached out to stroke the muzzle of the long rifle. She would protect her daughter—or die trying.

"Do not worry about that. They won't try that trick at night," Mack said confidently before turning to the first loophole.

Despite Mack's assurance, she was worried for him, too. She wasn't sure of her feelings for him yet, wasn't sure she wanted to have feelings for him, but she wasn't ready to lose him either. "Why not? It would be as simple as smoking bees from a hive."

He grinned and stroked the barrel of his rifle. "Not at night when we could see them in the dark for carrying the blazing torches and could pick them off as easily as shooting fish in a barrel."

Becca admitted she would prefer his description to hers, but she couldn't stop the swell of fear from building inside her. She had come so close to losing Caroline. . . . "I am going to check on Ruth and the children."

Mack caught her arm before she could take more than a step. "I doubt they have changed any from the last time you checked on them, and that was but a few moments ago. If anything was amiss, Reuben would have called for you."

Becca hefted the bag of lead shot and considered laying it against the side of Mack's head, but she knew he was right. She sighed. "I cannot stand the waiting, the uncertainty."

"It is hard, hard on all of us, but take pity on Reuben. He probably has the children settled down now, and you will only cause another disruption."

Mack was right, but that did not mean she had to like it. "He should not have to worry over the children when there is Ruth to consider."

"How is she?" Mack asked as he returned to his watchful position.

"She was sleeping."

"That's good."

"Yes, but she sleeps so deeply it is frightening. I know it worries Reuben. It worries me." Becca fingered the bag of powder again as she leaned in to look at one of the loopholes. She half wished an Indian would step into view just so she would have some way of fighting back against her fear. "I am afraid."

"Do not fear for her. Ruth is a strong woman, and she is a fighter. She loves her husband and her child too much to give up on life now. She's no quitter, and neither are you, Rebecca Wallace."

"Wouldn't do me much good if I were; it is not as if I could leave now."

Mack could hear the fear in her voice. He wanted to reach out to comfort her, but held back. He was afraid once he held her in his arms again he would never be able to let go. And that couldn't be.

"Would you, if you could?" As soon as the words were out of his mouth, Mack wished them back. It was a stupid question. What sane person would want to be holed up in a station with death knocking at the gate?

"No. There is too much here that is important to me."

There was a flicker of pleasure at the thought he

was important to her, but the sensation of fear was stronger. He could not let her become important to him. There was too much danger in that. He already cared too much—and he would pay the price for it. He could not afford to care still more. He could not afford the price *she* would have to pay for his love. "Don't."

"Don't what?"

"Don't care about me." Just the idea angered him. He didn't like losing control of his emotions, and yet that was exactly the sensation Rebecca Wallace seemed to inspire in him. He wouldn't tolerate it.

"Mack, you cannot stop it with words."

She studied him for a long moment, and he half feared, half anticipated she would reach for him, but she did not. Instead, she turned to peer out a loophole. He stood, watching her, and wished she had reached for him.

"Mack!" When she did grab his arm to pull him close, Mack knew she was no longer thinking as a lover. The fear in her voice, the painful grip of her fingers on his arm, sent that message clearly.

But when he put his eye to the loophole, the clearing surrounding the station had not changed from the last time he had looked.

Becca fumbled for the long rifle propped against the cabin wall. "Why aren't you shooting?"

"There is nothing there, Becca." Mack lifted his head from the loophole and pushed the rifle back down. His anger with her ebbed away as the need to comfort, to protect, asserted itself.

"But there was." She wrapped her arms around

herself. "There was an Indian there. I didn't imagine it."

"I believe you, but he is gone now."

"Why are they toying with us?"

"I don't know what is afoot, but we must be careful so we do not let them determine how we will act."

"It is too late for that." Becca's bitterness was apparent in her voice. "We are doing nothing but waiting for them to make the next move."

"That is not so easy a thing to do, at least while remaining aware. That, in a nutshell, may be their purpose."

"To have us die of nerves?"

Mack smiled. No matter how desperate the circumstances, he could always count on Becca's spirit to see her through. "That would serve their cause, but they may be waiting for us to let down our guard or even try to make a run for Boonesborough."

"Which we might have done if not for Ruth's labor."

She brightened so at the idea, he hated to continue his thought, but was more opposed to the idea she wouldn't be prepared for the worst.

"It could also be that they, too, are waiting."

"Waiting? For what?"

"Reinforcements."

A shudder went through her, and she stepped up to peer through the loophole as if afraid the reinforcements would appear with the very word. "So you do not think the war band we've been warned about is out there?"

"If that was the case, we would have been overrun long before."

"Will they come here?"

"I do not expect so. They've got bigger fish to net, but that does not mean we won't get swept up with the rest."

"What will become of us, Mack?" Her eyes seemed impossibly wide in her pale face.

"You need not fear, Becca. I will watch out for you." He would die for her if necessary. He could not love her, dared not love her, but he could protect her, would protect her.

She met his gaze. "But who will watch over you?"

He moved back to the loophole so he did not have to meet her eyes—or let her read his. "Do not concern yourself with me; you have enough to worry over."

"You cannot stop me from caring simply by wishing it," she said softly.

"I can and I will." He would make her see reason—one way or another.

She laughed. "And to think I once thought you knew much of women."

"I admit I know nothing of you." He stiffened his backbone, knowing he was again losing control of the situation.

"Do not short yourself. You know a great deal." She touched his arm. "But I also know a great deal about you. I know you care for me, just as I care for you."

He fought against the tremor of need her touch sent through him. He could not care about her. He could not destroy her. "Do not make more of this than there is."

"Do not make it less."

"This is not the time." He turned to give her a fierce glare to emphasize his point.

She didn't even flinch at his anger; instead, she reached up to stroke his face. "This is exactly the time. We are alone, we must stay alert and yet there is no focus for our minds. Most important, if we do not talk now, there may not be another chance."

How well he knew that! "There is nothing to discuss."

"Are you calling my feelings nothing?" The tremble in her voice shook him. He couldn't ignore her pain even if it served his purpose. He couldn't use her suffering to push her away—even if it was the best thing for her.

"Becca, you are confusing gratitude with something more. You will see."

"What I feel for you is not gratitude," she said with a quiet dignity more shattering than her tears.

There were so many layers to this woman, he could never hope to learn them all. Mack tried to tell himself that was the source of his fascination with her, but he knew it was a lie. What he felt for Rebecca Wallace was far more, and far deeper, than mere fascination.

"It must be."

She smiled gently. "I am grateful to you, for protecting my daughter and me, but this other is not something I welcomed either. I wasn't prepared to like a man, let alone feel something more, so I can understand why you are fighting it.''

"You do not understand.''

"Then, help me understand.'' Her chin lifted, and her face set into that familiar look of determination.

"It has nothing to do with you.''

Tears sparkled in her eyes, but she did not back down. "I think it has everything to do with me.''

"Then, you are wrong.'' He deliberately turned his back on her. It was one of the hardest things he had ever done, but he couldn't encourage her feelings for him. He had to put a stop to it now before it went too far—and she ended up dead as a result of him. "Maybe it would be best if you went to check on the children and Ruth.''

"No. You were right about that. I'm sure Reuben has things well in hand. I will go keep watch with Tad.''

That drew his attention away from the loophole. "You'll do no such thing. It is too exposed up there. You could be hurt.''

"It is no more dangerous there than here, and in case I must remind you, that is not your concern. You don't need to worry yourself about me.''

"I won't let you go up there. It's not safe.''

A flush of anger stained her cheeks as she glared at him. "You won't let me? How can you have any say over what I do?''

"I am responsible for your safety.''

"No longer. I won't hold you responsible, Mack. It's obviously too great a burden for you.''

* * *

Tad gave her a long study when she joined him in the tower. Blessedly he said nothing about her pink nose and tear-brightened eyes as he made room for her to lie beside him.

As the shadows lengthened and the sun dipped below the trees, Becca's soul eased, and she took comfort from his silence—strong and deep, so like his father's.

Just thinking about Cutter strengthened her resolve to reach through Mack's wall of rejection. If those close to him were certain about his feelings for Becca, then how could she believe his protests? And yet, part of her rebelled at the idea that she would have to fight him to admit his feelings and even made her question her own tentative beliefs. How could she care about a man? Especially a man so hardheaded as that.

With a sudden, sure movement Tad lifted his rifle and pulled off a shot into the gray light. He shook his head at Becca's questioning look. "I don't think I hit anything, but there is something going on out there, just look."

She strained her eyes and saw what drew his eye, more shadows flickering along the tree line. There was just enough light for her to know there were men there, lurking, hiding, but she could not pick out anything of substance.

She raised her own rifle and pulled off a shot as Tad reloaded his gun. Cutter poked his head through the trap door and touched his son's shoulder.

"Hold your fire."

"Pa, don't you see them out there?"

"I see them." Cutter's mouth was drawn into a tight line as he gazed past Becca's shoulder. "But I know if you hit one, it will be pure luck. We can't afford to waste shot and powder by shooting at shadows."

"But, Pa!"

"Hold your fire until you can be sure of your target."

When Tad subsided into sulky silence, Cutter turned his attention to Becca. "You best come below."

CHAPTER 19

"He's gone?" Becca repeated Cutter's words before pushing past him to rush down the ladder into the kitchen. It couldn't be true. She couldn't have understood him. Not even Mack would be that foolhardy. Not even Mack would want to die to prove a point.

Yet there was a hollow feeling in her center that only seemed to grow larger when she dropped to the kitchen floor from the ladder. It wasn't until she saw Reuben standing in the spot where she had left Mack, only a few hours before, that she finally understood—and believed. The hollow grew larger until she wobbled on her legs, steadying herself by putting a hand to the table.

He was gone.

Anger steadied her as she turned on Cutter, her

fists raised. "How could you let him go? How could you? He'll die out there and he won't know—"

She couldn't finish the sentence, not with Reuben standing there and Tad peeking through the drop door. Cutter seemed to understand and pulled her into a rough embrace, ignoring her fists and blaze of anger. She stood stiffly within the circle of his arms and knew the truth at last.

She didn't just have feelings for Mack. She loved him. There was no joyous swell of happiness at the idea. Only pain, worry, grief, and fear. Overwhelming fear. She didn't want to love him.

Something broke loose inside her, and suddenly she was weeping against Cutter's chest, as great, wracking sobs shook her. She took comfort from the soothing words he murmured in her ear and the gentle touch of his hand on her hair, but felt empty inside and alone, so alone, because he was not the man she loved.

After a time, Becca was finally able to take control of herself once more. She pulled away from Cutter and went to wash her face. When she returned to the cabin, she tried to smile away the worried look he gave her. "Do not worry. I am better now. I won't lose control again."

He couldn't mask the relief in his eyes, but said softly, "You are welcome to cry on my shoulder whenever you like."

"Why did you let him go?" Even knowing that Mack was a grown man that Cutter could not have stopped, Becca couldn't keep the hint of accusation from her voice.

"He chose his time very well." Cutter glanced at Reuben, who stood keeping watch at the loopholes.

The black man turned and gave Becca an apologetic look. "It my fault, miss. He told me what he was about, and I said he was a fool who'd get kilt if he didn't watch his back, but I didn't stop him. I went and told Mr. Cutter, but he too late to stop 'im. Mr. Mack was gone."

Reuben's words echoed horribly in her mind. A fool who would get killed. She knew Mack had deliberately chosen Reuben to tell of his plans, knowing the former slave wouldn't argue with a white man, even if he was headed for certain death, even if the man was his friend.

Cutter touched her shoulder. "Mack is a good scout. He's the best woodsman I've ever seen among white men and that includes Daniel Boone."

"That might comfort me if I thought he was going up against Boone, but it is the red men I am worried about. How does he compare with them?"

"He is very good," Cutter repeated.

The fact that he would not meet her eyes told Becca all she needed to know. Her stomach tightened into a knot of fear. There was only a slim chance that Mack would survive the night.

"Why don't you go join Emily with Ruth and the children? Go get some rest."

Becca shook her head. "I won't be able to rest. Not while he's out there."

"You are tired; I can see it in your face." He

touched her chin up so he could study her eyes. "You were up most of last night with Ruth. You need your rest."

"Don't ask that of me, Cutter." Her breath hitched. She paused to compose herself, knowing too much emotion would scarcely win her battle. "I couldn't bear sitting in that cabin and waiting for word. Let me go back up and keep watch with Tad."

Cutter hesitated, but finally nodded his approval. "You keep watch with Tad. Maybe you can take turns napping."

"That is a good idea," Becca said as she mounted the ladder, knowing full well she would not do any such thing.

It was the longest night of Becca's life. She swept her gaze across the open fields immediately surrounding the station, studying each shadow and movement in the pale moonlight with careful scrutiny, straining her ears for any sound that would give her a hint about their attackers or Mack. Every so often, she or Tad would catch a flicker of man-shaped shadows along the tree line, but true to Cutter's orders, they did not fire because they could not be sure of their shot.

"It will be light soon," Tad whispered as he stretched and shifted his weight, trying to ease into a more comfortable position.

Becca rubbed her eyes, trying to soothe their dry grittiness, but knew nothing short of sleep would help her now. Tad was right. The darkness had become more gray than black, and in the east there was just a hint of light beyond the trees to indicate the sun would rise soon.

"Everything quiet?" Tad asked softly.

Becca nodded. "Too quiet. I do not trust it."

They sat in companionable silence as the sun rose slowly. The smell of frying bacon wafted up through the trapdoor, and Tad's stomach growled. He gave Becca a sheepish look, and she smiled back at him, all the while wondering if she would ever be hungry again.

Suddenly rifle shots shattered the morning calm, and a man, featureless, nothing but a black shape in the glare, walked out of the morning sun.

Tad raised his rifle to his shoulder.

Becca's heart did a traitorous leap, and she put out her hand to push the barrel skyward. "No! It's Mack."

"How can you know?" Tad gave her a skeptical look, but did not aim his gun at the man again.

Becca couldn't tell him how she knew. Maybe it was the way he walked, the set of his shoulders, but when the man neared the station gate and they could see clearly that Becca had been right, she was not surprised.

Cutter called out to Tad to keep his eye out for trouble and rushed to admit Mack. No sooner was his friend within the walls, than Cutter slammed the gate shut and barred it once again.

"You are a damned fool, Silas McGee, but I'm glad to see you are still in one piece with your hair intact!"

Becca bit down on her lower lip until she tasted blood, but she didn't feel the sting of pain. Her entire being was focused on the man she loved.

"You may as well call your watch off for now." Mack glanced up quickly and looked away without meeting Becca's gaze. "They've gone."

Tad gave a whoop and swung down through the trapdoor. Becca stood in the tower, her feet rooted to the planks, her hands gripping the railing until her fingers ached.

"Gone?" Cutter echoed, running his fingers through his hair. "We're safe?"

"For now," Mack said grimly. "They pulled out during the night. I don't know where they went."

"How many were there? How can you be sure they are gone?"

Mack gave him a tired smile. "There were never more than a handful out there, and they went off as one. I watched them go and followed some distance."

"Were they heading for Boonesborough?"

"No. They were going north."

"So they may be heading out of Kentuck?" Cutter glanced at the kitchen doorway where Emily stood, hope etched on his face.

"They may."

"But you don't think so?"

Mack gave his friend a level look. "They didn't come all this way to spend a night to frighten us for no purpose. You know that as well as I."

"So what is the purpose?"

"I don't know."

Mack followed Cutter into the stable as they continued to discuss the Indians' intentions. Becca remained in the tower, still gripping the railing. She had thought he had risked himself for her. It was not what she wanted from him, his death in return for her protection, but she had welcomed that sign of his feelings for her.

Now she couldn't be certain of anything. Why hadn't he given her some sign? Why did she care? How could she love this man?

Twilight had fallen by the time Mack woke. He lay still and tried to decide what he would do next. He sensed the danger wasn't over and yet didn't want to do anything but stand watch. Just the thought of having nothing to do, but think of Becca, twisted his stomach into knots.

He could go out and scout again, but he doubted it would be so easy to escape the station this time. He was certain Cutter and Emily would have something to say about such foolhardy behavior. They would call it a suicide mission.

How could he explain that his life didn't matter?

He washed and dressed before making his way to the kitchen. He feared to find Becca there, but knew he had to eat. He needed to keep his strength up for what was ahead. He must stay strong to protect what mattered: his friends, their children, Becca.

The kitchen was empty, with only Tad above in the tower keeping watch. Mack watched with him as he ate cold biscuits and bacon, too restless to sit down, even to eat.

The swish of a full skirt in the dog trot, between

the kitchen cabin and the cabin that housed Cutter's family, brought him hurriedly down the ladder before he had time to form a conscious thought.

It was not Becca.

Emily made a face at him. "She is in our cabin with the babies. I convinced her that even with the rest she got today, she was better off taking it easy for a few days. She cannot tire herself out so much that her milk dries up. I don't know what we would do to feed two babies."

"Ruth is no better?" Mack asked, grasping at any topic that did not involve Becca. Just the mention of her name . . .

"She is still weak and feverish. I don't like the way it keeps coming back. Becca fixed a potion for her that breaks the fever, but it doesn't drive it away entirely."

"She is good with herbs. I doubt I would have survived my wound if not for Becca." He couldn't help himself. He wanted to say her name. *God help him. God help her.* She had saved his life. He would not return that gift by causing her death, but his desire for her made his chest ache. Even knowing he was the worst thing that could happen to her, he wanted her.

Emily gave him a sympathetic look. "Go to her, Mack. Tell Becca how you feel."

Becca. He needed her. The certainty of that need shook him to his soul.

He needed her. But if he took her, he would destroy her.

"I cannot." He tightened his mouth.

"Cannot or will not?" Emily studied him for a moment. "I never took you for a fool before, but you are doing a fair imitation of one these past days."

Mack had sat in the kitchen for a long time after she left him. He didn't remember making a decision, only knew that he had made one when he realized he was standing outside the cabin door. He knocked gently, telling himself he wanted only to make sure Becca was all right. She was his responsibility. He needed to know she was safe.

He needed.

All was so quiet within he almost moved away; but then the heavy wooden door swung open; and she stood there, framed by candlelight.

She had been crying. He could stand anything but that. The pain in her eyes broke through his resolve. He took her in his arms, and she fit against him as if she had been made for it. "What is it, my heart?"

"I am so afraid." She shivered, and he held her closer, warming her against his body, even though he knew she was not cold.

"I've never known you to let fear control you. You have the heart of a lion."

"I'm not afraid for me, but for them. They depend on me." She gestured to the cradle where the two bundled babies slept. "What if I cannot protect them?"

"Becca, you must know I will give my life to protect you and the children."

She shuddered and reached up to cup his face in her hands. "Don't, Mack. Don't say it. I want your protection, for the children if not for me, but I don't want it at any cost. Most especially not the cost of your life. That price is too high."

His mouth twisted into a smile. "My life is not worth much. I would consider it a worthy price."

"Why, Mack? Why is your life so worthless to you?"

His back stiffened, but she was so close, her eyes so full of love, he could not lie to her. Maybe if he told her the truth, she would finally understand. Certainly she would not look at him with anything more than disgust, unless it was pity.

"If you want to hear this story, then you best sit down."

She checked on the sleeping babies as she passed their cradle and then settled on the hearth rug before the fire. He crouched beside her, poking at the small fire with a stick, and tried to form the words that would kill her love for him.

As Mack told her about that winter morning when he and his father returned from a hunting trip to find their home burned and the rest of their family slaughtered, his voice tore at her heart. If she wasn't already in love with him, the pain in his voice would have bound her to him. As it was, she finally understood his devotion to duty, his need to protect, his drive to give recompense. All because a fourteen-year-old boy had begged his father to take him on a hunting trip.

She opened her mouth to tell him that it was not his fault, that if he had stayed at home with his mother, he would be as dead as the rest of his family, but she was certain he knew that. She knew others had told him as much, had reasoned with his head. Just as she knew, with the certainty of a woman who loved, that the only way to reach him was with her heart.

His attention was so fixed on the fire that he started when she touched him.

"Now you know the worst of what I am." His voice was so bleak it broke her heart.

She rose to her knees and drew him to her. When she kissed him, with fierce hunger, he answered with a passion that rocked her back. She clung to him as the need to love him, to be loved by him, swept through her, and she knew that no matter what, she would never let him go again.

When she ran her hands up beneath his shirt, tracing the lean contours and muscles of his flat stomach and broad chest, Mack made a low growl deep in his throat before pulling the shirt off and throwing it into a corner of the cabin.

Firelight shimmered over smooth muscles as he reached for her again. His clever lips traced her throat and teased her ear while his hands loosened her bodice and skirt. When he eased her back on the hearth rug, Becca wore nothing but her shift. The cotton had never felt so rough against her skin as she ached for his touch, his possession.

He left his breeches on as he greedily possessed her mouth again, the slick heat of his tongue teasing and probing her depths until she felt her blood pool hot and thick wherever his hands touched her, tracing the curve of her waist and swell of her hip, skimming down her thighs and then back up again, brushing her shift past her waist. He lifted her, and then the shift was gone, and she was naked before him. She reached for the laces of his breeches, and he pushed her hands away.

His hot lips traced the column of her throat and the valley between her breasts and the soft curve of her belly. When he moved between her spread legs, she didn't know what he meant to do, but she had given him her trust. There was nothing else to lose.

When those long fingers smoothed up the inner curve of her thighs, Becca felt a surge of heat and moisture at her core, and the need to be possessed made her raise her hips to meet his seeking hands. When the soft pressure of his lips followed the path his fingers had started, Becca thought she would die from wanting.

She ached.

She needed.

Then his hot tongue thrust to meet the ache and tease the bud of need, and she wept in desperation, digging her fingers into his shoulders. The pressure broke in a torrent that swept her with it as she cried out for Mack.

He answered her with a kiss, and this time when her hands moved to his laces, he let her untie them and help him ease his breeches off. However, when she would have pulled him down to her, he resisted.

"Remember the promise I made you? You will take me." He sat up and drew her onto his lap, spreading her legs wide so she would wrap them around his waist. "You will be in charge."

"I remember." She reached down between them to caress his thick staff, thrilling to the feel of its satin heat, and guided him to her. The need he had satisfied only moments before returned with a rush as the tip of his shaft touched her and she opened to him. "I want you inside me."

Mack gripped her hips as he drove into her. His tongue probed the depths of her mouth until Becca lost track of all knowledge but the sensation of slick, hot need building within her. Then her body clenched around him with tight, convulsive release, and he cried out her name against her mouth.

When he eased her gently to lay her back against the hearth rug, Becca pulled him with her. She traced the rippling muscles of his arms and smoothed her hands across his shoulders to touch his face. "I love you."

She felt him tense beneath her touch, but he did not pull away. Such a little thing to be grateful for.

A shadow dimmed his eyes. "God help me. I love you, Becca. God help you."

The pain on his face took the pleasure out of the moment for her. "Why is that such a bad thing, Mack?"

He met her gaze with a tortured look. "How can you ask that after what I just told you?"

"What did you tell me?" She couldn't quite keep the tremble from her voice, but didn't dare to wait to steady herself. It was too important to reach him now, now before it was too late, before he took one reckless chance too many. "Bad things happen, Mack. I know that better than most people, but it seems you have not learned that lesson yet for all you know about life. Bad things happen, and they are no one's fault. Certainly not yours."

"I can't promise you a future I don't have."

CHAPTER 20

I can't promise you a future I don't have.

Becca returned Mack's serious gaze and tried not to flinch. "I believe you can have a future, if you let yourself live, and be happy. Can you do that?"

"I'm happy right now. Can't we let that be enough?"

It was not enough, not when she had finally begun to believe that tomorrow was a promise and not a threat; but she was still learning to take each moment of joy as it came, and so she went into his arms and did not bring up love and the future again.

The babies woke them during the night, hungry and wet. While Becca fed Caroline, whose cries were the most insistent, Mack surprised her by changing the newborn.

He smiled at her astonishment. "I've more experience than your average bachelor, but then, that should not be a surprise to anyone who knows Emily. She does not consider caring for children exclusively women's work and will press any pair of hands into service when necessary. I changed Ima's linens more than once when she was a baby, and I doubt this will be the last time I change this little one."

Caroline's hunger sated, Becca took the smaller baby from Mack. Running her hand gently over the downy black curls, she gave the tiny girl a breast. "I hope Ruth will be able to nurse her soon. If not, her milk will dry up. I would hate for her to miss this special time with her baby."

"Will you stay here if she needs you?" Mack asked quietly.

Surprised, she raised her gaze to meet his. "I will stay as long as they need me." It was unusual for Mack to speak of the future. She wondered what he was thinking. Then she knew. He only wanted to make sure she was settled. Safe and secure in a home that he did not have to provide. Her eyes filled with tears.

He looked away and tended to Caroline's needs before tucking the baby back into the cradle. When the newborn finished her midnight snack, he gently laid her snugly beside Caroline.

Then he led Becca back to their blanket before the dying fire and made tender love to her. With each gentle touch, each soft word, she fell deeper in love with him, and her heart broke.

After making love to Becca, he kissed her and tasted her tears in surprise. "Did I hurt you?"

"No," she whispered brokenly, turning her face into his shoulder.

He could feel her hot tears against his skin. Her silent weeping cut him to the quick, and he tightened his arms around her. The need to protect her filled him. "Why are you crying?"

"I am so happy I want this moment to last forever, and I know it will not, because you are saying good-bye."

She spoke the truth, but her quiet words still caused him pain. "You knew from the beginning there would be no forever with me."

Her sigh tickled his skin. "I knew, but I never knew how hard it would be to let you go. I never dreamed I would want a man, let alone love him. I never thought I would want a future with a man, but I do, Mack. Only you don't believe in the future."

Her words, her pain, tore at his heart, and he knew he had been right. He should never have let himself love Becca, let her love him, and yet he would not trade these quiet moments in her arms for anything.

Long after she slept, he lay awake, watching her, memorizing her face. She was wrong. He believed in the future, but he knew it held nothing good for him. As bleak as he had always expected his future to be before, it would be even more desolate and empty without Becca in it. Even after he fell asleep, he slept lightly, so he heard Reuben's quiet tap on the door and went out into the early morning mist to talk with the man without waking Becca.

Mack knew what his friend's news was before he

spoke a word. Reuben's wide smile and bright eyes
told all.

"Ruth is better today?" Despite his heavy heart,
Mack couldn't help smiling in answer to Reuben's
obvious joy. It was uplifting to have some good news,
to know someone looked forward to the future.

"She woke up this mornin', and the first thing she
want to know is where her baby is. She says she's
bursting and needs to nurse, so I come for the baby."

"I'm glad, Reuben." Mack squeezed his shoulder.
"I'll go get your daughter."

He had thought Reuben's smile couldn't grow any
bigger, but when the large man took his tiny daughter
into his arms, his grin widened impossibly. "You
thank Miss Becca for me, won't you? For taking care
of her?"

"I'll do that. Now you go take care of your women-
folk."

Reuben winked at him. "And you see to your'n."

When Mack closed the door, he saw Becca was
awake. She sat up, clutching a blanket to hide her
nakedness, but her smooth shoulders were bare, and
the curve of one creamy breast drew his eye. She had
never looked more beautiful, with her hair tousled
and her lips swollen from making love to him. He
wanted her all over again.

"It has come."

She gave his look of confusion a small, sad smile.
"The morning. I never thought I would dread it so
much."

He knelt beside her. "It is not good-bye."

"Not yet. That is what you mean, is it not? But it

will be soon, I know it." Her mouth trembled. "I feel it."

He didn't know what to say to her and was saved by Caroline's petulant cry. When she bent over her nursing daughter, the long fall of her hair nearly hid her face from view, but not so much that he missed the sparkle of tears in her eyes.

"Don't cry. Please don't cry over me; it tears me up inside." He leaned closer and put his arms around her, touching his lips to the top of her head.

She relaxed against him for a moment before pulling away. "I know. I'm sorry. Can you give me some time to myself? I will pull myself together, so you don't need to see my tears, but I need a few moments."

And so he was keeping watch, allowing Cutter time to breakfast with his family, when the riders came. He recognized enough of the men to know they came from Boonesborough and that they had brought trouble with them.

Tension was thick as the residents of Cutright's Station gathered around the newcomers and listened to their news.

"It's come, but not the way we thought." Joe Miller, a red-haired mountain of a man with fists the size of hams, paced before Cutter as he talked. "That big war party we've all been afearing is in Kentuck all right, but it didn't hit Boonesborough like we thought. They've got Bryan's Station under siege right now. We're riding to help them out and don't have time to waste. Are you with us?"

"There was a group here the night before last,"

Cutter said quietly. "They didn't do much but make certain we didn't leave."

Miller nodded. "They was doing that all around. More than a half dozen stations in all. Only one man got shot out of the deal, and he was shot by his own son who got a mite trigger happy. We reckon they was trying to split us up so no one would offer help when they finally settled on a target."

"And we're certain they've settled on a target?" Cutter asked.

"Boone is. He's heading there now." Miller spat and mounted again. "I've had my say. Are you coming?"

"Pa! More friendlies coming in. Otter and Big Fist."

"I don't know that I believe Indians got it in 'em to be friendly." Miller spat again as he eyed Cutter.

Mack knew there was a reason he had never liked the man.

"These do. They are my friends, and I won't stand for someone even talking about harming them." Cutter's voice was soft, almost gentle, but the hard glare he gave Miller sent his threat loud and clear.

Miller was the first to look away. "So you riding or socializing with your friends?" He managed to deliver his question with a sneer.

Cutter smiled. "I'll wait to hear what my friends have to say before I make any decisions."

"I ain't waiting. Come when you're ready, if you're ready." He spurred his horse out the gate before Cutter could respond to the dig.

Otter and Big Fist trotted through the gates before

the dust from the riders had cleared. The two Indians confirmed the attack on Bryan's Station.

"This is the English last try to take this land. If you drive them out now, they not be back," Big Fist told them. "There be much fighting. They've taken all for this attack. There no danger here."

Cutter met Mack's eyes even as Emily took her husband's arm, his name a plea on her lips.

Mack knew better than to look at Becca. Her pain would not change his mind, but it would make it harder to leave.

"I'll go," he said. "You stay here, Cutter."

"They'll need every able man to drive off a force this size." Cutter touched his wife's cheek. "I've got to go."

Mack shook his head. "You stay here with your family, Cutter."

"Pa, I'll go with Mack. You stay here with Em." Tad stepped up, holding his lanky frame tall, his shoulders squared manfully. He had never looked so young and vulnerable to Mack.

"Tad, I need you here to watch out for the women-folk. Reuben can't do it alone. Mack and I will go to settle this once and for all."

Emily bit down on a knuckle, her face pale, as Cutter led her to their cabin to pack his gear together.

Becca followed Mack to the stable where he started to saddle Joseph. He avoided meeting her eyes because he didn't want to face the pain he knew he would find there. "Don't try to talk me out of this. I'm going. I have to do this. For you."

"For me! You are going off to get yourself killed

for me. That is rich." She gave a short, humorless laugh.

He turned to face her, glad to see the light of anger in her eyes. Anger, he could face; it was her fear that undid him.

"I am doing it for you, because if we can win this battle, this may be the message the British need to know that Kentucky cannot be taken from the Americans." He gripped her shoulders and met her gaze so she could read his intent in his eyes. "I am doing this for you, so you can live."

"So I can live. . . ." She widened her eyes. "That's what you're afraid of, isn't it? Living. You say you don't want to die, but that's what you have been doing ever since that day you found your family dead. Now you've finally got a chance to be alive—to live—and you are too afraid to take it."

"You don't understand," he said stiffly and released his hold on her so he could step back.

She laughed bitterly. "I understand perfectly. I understand you so well I know you are going to ride off and break my heart rather than admit I'm right— that I am braver than you. After all, even knowing everything I know about life and love and men, I'm willing to risk it all for you, yet you are so stuck in the past, so determined to pay for someone else's mistake, you won't take that chance with me."

"Becca, I—"

She held up her hand. "Don't bother to make excuses. I'll do it for you. Go, ride, and damn you to hell for making me love you."

* * *

Becca sat in the tower, the long rifle cradled in her arms like a baby, and watched. Behind her, someone opened the trapdoor and placed something on the floor before climbing through. The trapdoor dropped back into place with a thud as Emily sat down beside her.

Becca kept watching the open land around the station, her eyes alert for any flicker of movement, and ignored the other woman. Emily took hold of the rifle, and only then did Becca turn to face her with narrowed eyes. "Let it be."

"You need to eat," Emily said quietly, but she released the gun.

"I need to keep watch. I'll eat when I get hungry."

"And when will that be?"

"I don't know, but worrying me about it isn't going to bring my appetite back now, is it?"

Something flashed in Emily's eyes, but she pressed her lips together. "You won't be much good to us, or your daughter, if you faint from hunger."

"I've gone longer than this without food. I can't think about food when I don't know. . . . We'll know soon enough."

"Starving yourself won't bring Mack back any faster."

Becca winced at his name. She didn't want to think about him. She couldn't stop thinking about him, worrying about him. "Neither will eating. I'm not hungry."

"I know how you are suffering. I understand." Emily touched her shoulder.

Becca flinched away. "No, you don't."

"We are both worried for our men—what is different?" Emily persisted.

Becca shuddered, remembering, and shook her head.

"He loves you. He will come back to you." Emily's voice was full of sincerity.

Narrowing her eyes, Becca focused on a slight movement at the tree line; but only a family of deer stepped through the trees to nibble at the field of corn, and she leaned back with a sigh.

Emily did not leave. "I care for him, too. He is a friend, no, more than a friend, as close as a brother. I worry for both of them. It would not take the pain away for us to worry together, but I've learned it helps to share the burden."

"If you care for Mack, then you will not want me to share your burden with you." Becca's lips felt stiff and awkward as she shaped the words.

"You love him."

"That doesn't matter."

"Of course it matters. Are you worried because you've not married yet?" Emily laughed. "I'm not the one to preach a sermon because a couple anticipated their wedding vows. Do not worry on that account."

"It was not a matter of anticipating those vows, for there will be no vows. Mack won't marry me."

"Yes, he will." Emily nodded to emphasize her point.

Becca shook her head. "You don't understand, Emily. He's not coming back. He rode out of here intending to die. I can only hope and pray that he does not take your husband with him."

CHAPTER 21

Mack came to himself suddenly. Screaming horses and Indian war cries clamored with shouting men and booming rifles in a cacophony of sound. The acrid stench of burnt powder almost overwhelmed the scent of fresh blood.

Through the haze of smoke hovering in the air, he could barely make out a pair of figures locked in mortal combat to his left. A splattering thud sounded as a war ax connected with a head, and one of the men slid to the ground, the side of his head caved in, as the other staggered off into the smoke, leaving Mack alone with the dead.

He knew he would soon be among them. He could feel his lifesblood oozing from his thigh and yet couldn't bring himself to care about his fate. Then he thought of Becca, and fear tore through him. He couldn't die until she was safe. Then he remembered. She was safe at Cutright's Station. Safe, for now.

Memories licked through his brain. Burned fields. Dead cattle with swollen bellies. Trampled corn. Gutted cabins. The vengeful Kentuckians pressing on from Bryan's Station without waiting for reinforcements, determined to stop the invading Indians from escaping north of the Ohio River to the safety of Indian territory. Then the trap just at the southern fork of the Licking River.

To his right he heard another man's pleas for mercy cut off by a gurgle as someone slit his throat, and Mack knew he was a dead man. Then the pain hit and drove him into blessed blackness again.

When he woke again the battle was over. A bottle fly crawled over the sticky blood on his left shoulder, which must have been the wound that drove him into unconsciousness. Mack knew better than to flick the fly away, even assuming he could raise his other arm to do so. Near at hand, he heard the desperate cries of a dying horse and the groans of an injured man, but there were also more surreptitious movements that made him hold still.

A moccasin scuffed in the dirt near his face, and Mack held his breath while tensing himself to battle for his life. The man knelt beside him, the fringe of his buckskins brushing Mack's shoulder.

"Damn you, Silas McGee. How am I going to tell Emily I let you get killed? What am I going to tell Becca?"

The grief in Cutter's voice stirred Mack.

"Just make sure you get home in one piece so you

can tell them yourself. They'll get over my death, but I'm afraid if you don't make it home in one piece, Emily will go to hell and back to strip a piece off my hide." Mack lay panting from the effort of speaking and wished he were dead. It would save them all a lot of trouble since he was sure he would die soon enough.

"If we don't get you out of here, but quick, she will have to go to hell to find either of us," Cutter said quietly. "Can you walk?"

"I'll do what I have to do."

Despite his assurance, Cutter did more carrying than Mack did walking, during their long trek off the Blue Licks Battlefield. He tried to help, but his right leg wouldn't support his weight, and leaning too much on his left arm caused fiery pain that led to blackouts. Several times he begged Cutter to leave him behind, knowing the other man could escape to safety and eventually go home to his family, but Cutter wouldn't leave him.

More than once they were discovered escaping, and Cutter had to let Mack fall painfully to the ground to fight and kill. Each blackout left Mack weaker, and he found it more and more difficult to fight his way back to consciousness. And then he fought no more.

When his eyes opened, Mack lay curled on his side, his head pillowed against a rock. He could feel more rock fitted all around him. Everything was black. Cutter had left him after all. Knowing his friend's deep sense of loyalty, he could think of only one reason Cutter would leave him behind.

Mack was glad to be dead. His only regret was that

he would never see Becca again. He knew Cutter would take care of her until she found a man who would love her the way she deserved, but that didn't stop the need, the wanting, the love.

Just the thought of her sent a stabbing pain through his heart, pain that seemed to echo the agonizing throbbing in his leg and twisting ache in his shoulder. He managed to think hazily that death wasn't as painless as he had been led to believe before blackness claimed him again.

"Mack, wake up! It's time to go." Cutter's voice cut through the darkness and shadows of pain. A rough hand shook his shoulder, and Mack groaned in response, trying and failing to twist away. There was no room to maneuver in the stony embrace.

"Go? Are you dead, too? I knew I would go, but I didn't think you would go to hell." Mack knew he was mumbling. His voice sounded strange to his ears, but he didn't really care.

Cutter drew up Mack's uninjured arm and draped it over his shoulder. "We've got to get moving. This sinkhole isn't safe anymore, not in full sunlight. There's a cave up ahead where we can hide until dark."

Mack shook his head, even though it made him more dizzy. "You've got your facts all wrong, Cutter. They don't have sun in hell, and you sure can't hide from the devil. I've been trying my whole life and look where it got me."

"Damn it, Mack. Don't give up on me now. Stay alert, man." Cutter hauled him out of his stone coffin with a grunt. "I'm going to get you home if it's the last thing I do or I really will go to hell."

"Home? Becca." Mack slid into unconsciousness again with her name on his lips.

Becca choked down another mouthful of corn bread and took a sip of buttermilk as Emily watched over her.

"You don't need to watch every mouthful go down." Becca scowled at the other woman.

"I do if I want to be certain you're eating. With Ruth just barely out of bed and scarcely fit to walk to the privy alone, let alone stand watch, I can't spare you time to be sick."

"And yet you can spare the time to nag me about eating," Becca snapped back, but quickly took another bite of corn bread to stop Emily from another comment.

"I always make time for the things that I enjoy." Emily smiled and filled Becca's mug to the brim before carrying the pitcher to the kitchen door. "See that you finish that buttermilk to the last drop. I'll know if you don't."

"She will, too. I can't hardly stir a finger before she's there to make sure I don't overdo." Ruth rocked slowly, her child nestled against her shoulder, sleeping soundly.

"You don't need to overdo when you've got your work cut out for you just telling tales on me."

Ruth's dark eyes gave her a steady look. "It ain't

a bad thing to have people care about you and fuss over you, Miss Becca.''

Ruth's quiet reprimand filled Becca with shame.

"I don't know why y'all bother with me. I'm more trouble than I'm worth. I might as well be a man."

Ruth laughed out loud, her deep belly chuckle causing her baby to stir in her sleep. "You ain't that much trouble yet, girl, but you gettin' close. Now finish that buttermilk up and go relieve my man in the tower. I've got just enough energy left to nag him, and I don't want to waste it.''

Becca finished her meal and climbed the ladder to the tower where Reuben leaned against the railing as he scanned the station's fields.

"I'll take over for now." She propped her long rifle against the rail and leaned companionably beside him. "You best go below. Ruth says she's got some nagging to do.''

"Maybe I best stay up here with you." Reuben gave Becca a sly grin.

"Not a chance of that. You're on your own. They've already had their go at me today. They practically counted every bite of food I put in my mouth.''

"Good." Reuben moved to the trapdoor and started down the ladder. "Mr. Mack don't like his women scrawny."

His laughter flowed up through the door before Becca slammed it shut. Only after she knew she was alone, did she let her lips curve into a smile. Ruth was right. It wasn't a bad thing to let people fuss over you. In fact, she had learned it left a warm glow to know that she wasn't so alone in the world after all.

However, turning back to the rail, which also offered a view of the closed and barred station gates, Becca couldn't stop the shiver of fear that traveled through her. She wasn't alone, but the fact that she now had others to care about only meant she had more concerns.

She had to worry that Ruth was recovering from her fever, that Reuben and Tad didn't take unnecessary risks as they scouted around the station, that Cutter and Mack would come home alive. That, most of all, caused her worry, because she had no way to know what had happened to them.

"Mack, come home to me," she whispered softly and prayed as she tried to forget those last bitter words she had stabbed at him, hoping to wound.

The days since the men had left for Bryan's Station were long and tiring. They still kept watch on the walls, but now their vigilance cost more, for there were fewer to stand watch and more to worry about. However, Becca's renewed sense of belonging made her all the more determined to be alert, especially because she was watching for more than signs of trouble.

When she saw the single rider break through the trees and head for the station gates, Becca's heart stopped. Then she recognized the lad who had brought them news of the war party, and the swell of hope and fear ebbed away, leaving only a heavy lump in her gut.

"Rider!" she called out and hurried below. She wanted to hear his every word for herself.

The boy's face was pale beneath his freckles. After

dismounting, he accepted the dipper of water from Emily and drank deeply before delivering his news. The reason for his pallor soon became clear.

The force attacking Bryan's Station had fled by the time the Kentucky reinforcements had arrived. The frontiersmen, angered by the wanton destruction, gave chase and fell into a trap near Blue Lick. Many Kentucky men were dead and wounded.

"My brother was sent on ahead to give word for those heading home." The boy gave Emily a level look. "He said to tell you that when he last saw your husband, he was whole and well."

Emily slid her arm around Becca's waist as she gave him a tremulous smile. "Thank you, but what of his partner, Silas McGee?"

The boy's eyes slid away. "I don't know."

Becca pulled away from Emily and stepped closer to the boy. She took his chin in her hand and forced him to meet her eyes. "Tell me what you know. It is better to know the worst than to only imagine it. Trust me on this."

"My brother said he saw him go down." The boy shuddered and closed his eyes for a moment as if imagining the horrors his brother had described on the battlefield. "But he didn't think he was dead, 'cuz he was cussing a blue streak."

"That sounds like our Mack." Emily drew Becca back to the protection of their small huddle.

"Thank you," Becca whispered.

Becca stood transfixed until the boy mounted and rode out. The slam of the bar locking the gate behind him jarred her out of her dark thoughts. She forced

her legs to take one step and then another, but Emily
caught her arm before Becca could even determine
which direction she wanted to take.

"He'll be home soon enough; Cutter will see to
that."

"Don't make promises you don't have the power
to keep," Becca said through stiff lips. Her whole
body felt stiff and cold, so cold. She wrapped her
arms around herself in a vain attempt to stay warm.

"You can't mean what you said to me that day in
the tower," Emily argued, folding her arms across
her chest. "You must know that is nonsense."

"It does not matter whether or not I believe it."
Becca sighed. She didn't have the energy to argue
with Emily. Didn't she understand nothing mattered
anymore? "What matters is whether or not Mack
believes it."

"Pish, posh. A man believes what you tell him to
believe."

"That may work for you, Emily, but I am not as
strong as you."

"Becca—"

"Excuse me. I have to go keep watch now."

CHAPTER 22

Becca woke with a start when a shaft of light struck her eyes. The cabin door stood open behind Ruth, whose smile seemed almost brighter than the noon-time sun. "They come home."

She was out of the door, brushing past Ruth, before Becca realized she was wearing only her shift, but then she caught sight of Mack and she didn't care. She fairly flew across the station yard, passing Cutter and Emily, who were wrapped in a passionate embrace, and dropped to her knees beside Mack.

Cutter had rigged up a travois that was hauled by the skinniest, knock-kneed pony she had ever seen. Mack lay beneath a tattered blanket that did little to cover him. His face was flushed beneath his tan, and he lay so still her breath hitched. Surely Cutter would have warned her if he had hauled home a corpse rather than a living man?

She stretched a hesitant hand to touch Mack's face. He was warm to the touch—too warm by far—but she was reassured. At least he was still alive.

"Mack, what have you done to yourself?" she whispered.

He opened his eyes and gave her a lopsided grin. "Hello, darling, you look good enough to eat, but I don't seem to have the strength to lift my arms, let alone love you like you deserve. . . ." His eyes closed again as his voice faded.

Frantic, Becca pressed her hand to his chest, fearing he had made it home to her only to die, but the reassuring beat of his heart satisfied her that was not the case.

She stood, determined that Mack would live, in spite of himself. "Tad, unhitch this beast before it topples over onto Mack. Reuben, Cutter, carry Mack inside before he wakes again. Ruth, go get those bandages and things we prepared. Emily, put water on to boil."

Without looking to see if the others obeyed her orders, Becca followed Reuben and Cutter into the cabin. "No, do not put him on the bed yet. Lay him on the table until we've tended him." She wrinkled her nose as she stepped around Cutter to reach the table. "While we're doing that, Stephen Cutright, you best take a bath as well."

Slipping Mack's knife from its sheath, she started slitting off his buckskins before she remembered that Cutter had been in the battle as well.

Turning, Mack's knife in hand, she looked the

other man up and down. "Are you fit? Do you need help?"

Cutter eyed the knife in her hand and backed toward the door. "No, ma'am, I've been washing myself pretty regularly for the past thirty years or so. I think I can manage on my own today."

Becca lowered the knife and smiled. "I know that, but I thought you might be hurt, too."

He smiled back. "I'm fine." His smile faded. "It's Mack that needs all your help now."

"Thank you for bringing him home safe." She turned back to Mack, and her smile faded as her grip tightened on the knife. Safe, but not sound.

He had only been gone a week, and yet Mack seemed thinner than she remembered. His skin stretched taut across muscle and bone as if his fever had burned all else away.

The source of the fever was immediately apparent as she inspected his wounds. Although the shoulder wound was bigger, a gaping hole blasted by a musket ball, it was the wound in his calf that was a swollen, angry red. It oozed pus when she pulled off the bandage, which had obviously been made of the tattered dirty blanket that had covered Mack on the travois.

Becca's mouth tightened at the sight.

"That is my fault," Cutter said grimly from the door. "I could not keep it clean, not when I had to drag him through the dust in a travois. I've likely killed him."

Reuben touched Cutter's shoulder. "No. He's too stubborn and hardheaded to die. You know that. The worst that will happen is he'll lose that leg."

"Stubborn he is." Cutter gave Becca a steady look. "You know why we pushed so hard to get back despite his injuries? He wanted to see you."

Cutter shook his head. "No. That's not right. He needed to see you. Half the time he was out of his head from pain and fever, but you were what brought him back. He lived just to see you again."

"I won't let him die now that he has."

"I know you won't, but you don't have to do it alone. Just remember, Becca, we all care for him, too."

She gave Cutter a fleeting glance before turning back to Mack.

Becca worked tirelessly to keep her word. She cleaned and bandaged his shoulder, then concentrated her efforts on the leg wound because she knew this would be where the battle for Mack's life would be won or lost.

She reopened the wound with a hot knife and scraped it clean while Cutter and Reuben held a tight-lipped Mack to the table. He never cried out, not even during the worst, but he bit down so savagely on the scrap of leather Emily gave him that the cords in his neck stood out in sharp relief. When he blacked out again from the pain, they were all relieved.

Becca packed the wound and bandaged it, then fed him broth and tea. She sat with him through the night, feeding him more tea when he stirred and battling the hot fever with cool water and angry prayers.

She paid no attention as the others came and went with some pattern they had determined on their own.

All she cared was that someone brought water, broth, bandages and herbs when she asked—no demanded. She had no patience for niceties and no attention for anything but Mack.

Sometime near dawn his fever raged higher than before, and her tears mixed with the water she cupped across his body trying to cool it. He felt so hot to the touch, she wondered steam didn't rise from him when the cool water touched his burning skin. She feared his very life was burning away.

It was Emily who battled with her as the sun started its ascent and Emily who held her when she cried helpless tears and Emily who touched Mack's cheek and felt the difference in his temperature. "Becca, it's worked! The fever is gone. You've won."

Becca stretched a hand toward Mack, but stopped just short of contact, for fear Emily was mistaken. "He's so still."

"He's sleeping," Emily said gently and put Becca's hand on Mack's chest where she could feel the cool skin and the thud of his heart beneath it.

"Poor man is tired. After all, he's been fighting death along with us. He will likely sleep for hours. It will be the best thing for him." Emily gathered up the cloths and basins they had been using. "I know it is the best thing for you, too. You know you pushed yourself too hard while he was gone, and now you've done it again. I'll not have you fall sick now just so I can have two invalids to care for."

"I'll not leave him." Becca set her chin at a defiant angle, and she sent Emily a glare. "He needs to know I'm here."

"Who said you had to leave him. You can lie down here beside him and sleep, too," Emily said soothingly as she guided Emily down on the corn-husk mattress. "Just sleep, Becca, and let time do its work on both of you."

"Becca."

The dry, rasping voice sounded in the darkness and struck fear into her heart. For a moment she thought death had come to claim Mack—and take her with it. Why else would it know her name? Then she felt him stir beside her, and she knew it was Mack calling for her.

"Becca."

"Hush, darling. Let me light a candle and then I will see to your needs." She brushed a kiss across his forehead, to reassure herself and soothe him, as she scrambled from the bed, and was relieved to feel he was still cool and unfevered.

They had slept the day away, she saw, and that explained the hollow feeling in her stomach. While they had slept, someone had brought in corn bread and a crock of broth that was still warm in its thick covered pot. Her stomach rumbled as she lifted the lid and the delicious aroma wafted out.

She dipped a tin cup in the bucket of water standing by the door and brought it to Mack. He smiled at her before drinking it down greedily.

"We need to talk, Becca."

Her hand shook as she went to refill the cup, but she had steadied herself by the time she returned to the bed. "After you've had your fill of water and broth. You must work to keep up your strength."

He moved to take the cup from her; but she could see how unsteady his hand was, from weakness not emotion as had been her trouble, and she put her hand over his to steady it while he drank.

"I was not sick all that long. How could I lose my strength so fast?" He scowled at her as if it was somehow her fault.

Becca smiled, just relieved to have him well enough to argue with her, and moved to scoop out a cup of broth. "You almost died, Mack. That is enough to drain the strength from anyone."

"I would not have died." His scowl deepened.

She raised her eyebrows. "You came very close."

"I thought I had died. When I was at Blue Licks."

Sitting on the edge of the bed, Becca touched him again just to reassure herself that he was alive.

"I thought I was in hell. That's where I'm going, Becca, you can be sure of it."

"I can't be sure of it, and neither can you." She held the cup to his lips. "Now drink this and stop all this nonsense."

He drank two cups of broth and waited patiently while she ate some corn bread and took some broth for herself. Becca ate slowly. Although she had been ravenous only moments before and filled with exuberance with the knowledge that Mack was going to live, now she was reluctant to have this conversation with Mack. She sensed she did not want to hear what he had to say to her.

"Becca." He looked at her, and she set the empty cup down with a heavy thunk.

"You almost died," she repeated stubbornly. "But you did not. Now is the time to think of living. Have you finally decided that you will allow yourself to live?"

She went to him and sat on the edge of the bed, hoping her nearness would remind him of all the reasons he had to live life to the fullest.

"I will live as I always have."

"That is not living," Becca said scornfully, refusing to reach for him when he would not close the inches between them to touch her himself. She knew he wasn't that weak. He had simply chosen not to do so. "If that is the way you plan to live, I don't know why I worked so hard to save your life—again."

"Because that is the way you are made."

His gentle voice grated on her nerves. How could he be so certain, so sure, this was his future?

"I wish you could learn to accept me for the way I am made."

"What I do not accept is the way you think you are made." Unable to sit still any longer, Becca paced the small stretch of plank flooring beside the bed. She placed her feet carefully, making sure to walk only on one long, wide board as if her life depended on balancing on that path. "You love me. You said so."

"I have nothing to give you, but my life. You deserve so much more."

There was regret in his voice. She tried to take some comfort from that, but couldn't.

"You are right." Her voice caught on the words. "I deserve to be loved. Why can't you love me?"

"Something broke inside me that day, Becca. I can't explain it any better than that."

"I think the reason you can't explain it is because you don't believe it any more than I do. You love me." Maybe if she repeated the words enough, they would get through to him.

"Yes. I do." He grimaced as if the idea made him uncomfortable. "But it's not enough."

She hoped he was uncomfortable. "So you can live without me?"

"I'll have to, won't I?"

"Tell me just one thing." She stopped her pacing to give him a searching look. "Why were you so determined to come back to me?"

That made him pause for a moment. "I don't know. I was out of my head."

"Maybe that should tell you something." She started pacing again. It was the only alternative to hitting an injured man. "Maybe you should stop listening to your head and start listening to your heart."

"I'm not out of my head anymore, Becca."

"I can't win." She was so tired. It was easier to fight the fever than his stubborn Scots' mind. "Can I?"

"No. I'm sorry." There was regret in his voice, but it wasn't enough for Becca. She didn't want regret from him. That was the last thing she wanted from him.

"I'm sorry, too, but not for what you think." Turning on her heel, she raised her gaze to meet his. "I'll never be sorry for loving you, because at least I can feel, and I can live. I'm sorry for you, Silas McGee, because you can't."

"I can and I do. I love you, Becca, never doubt that."

"How can you love me and hurt me this way? How can you say you love me?" She ached with the effort not to cry, her entire body tensed with the effort to stop her heart from breaking, because she knew the pain would tear her apart. She had survived beatings and Indian raids and torture, but she wasn't at all certain she could survive this. "How can you?"

"I don't know." He whispered her name, as soft as a prayer, his hands convulsing against the quilt and then reaching out for her. "But I do love you. I would die for you."

"I don't want that, Mack. I don't want that at all." She shied away from his touch, knowing it would destroy her the way her husband's brutal fists had not. "I only want you to live for me."

"I can't give you that."

CHAPTER 23

"You want to do what?" Cutter drove his knife into the butcher block with unnecessary force, pitched the chunk of wood he had been carving into the fire, causing a shower of sparks, and turned on Becca with a glare.

She swallowed nervously, but stood her ground. She had thought too long and hard about this to back down now. It hadn't been an easy decision to come to, not when going back to Virginia would likely put her back within reach of her stepfather, who might very well try to marry her off to another brute.

But she hadn't felt there was much choice. Not when Mack was in Kentucky. She would rather stand up to her stepfather than battle against Mack's need to die, or to watch Mack die. She swallowed again. "I want to go to Boonesborough. Tomorrow. I know you just returned home, Cutter, so if you don't want to leave, then Tad and Reuben can take me. If you can't spare them, all I ask is the loan of a horse."

"Tomorrow?" Cutter repeated.

Giving her husband's obvious confusion a gentle smile, Emily shook her head, but the look she turned on Becca was anything but gentle. "I never took you for a coward, Becca."

Becca folded her arms across her chest. "I am not. He won't have me, and I won't stay here with him—" Unable to finish her sentence, she turned her head to hide the tears sparkling in her eyes.

"Of course, you should not have to. Tomorrow," Cutter said softly, "tomorrow I will take you to Boonesborough."

"Thank you," Becca said, forcing a small smile of gratitude, hardly daring to allow herself that much emotion for fear it would all, everything she felt, come pouring out in a rush of pain.

"Coward."

"Emily!" Cutter gave his wife a reproving glance.

She ignored it, focusing on Becca. "What else can it be, but cowardice? You are leaving when he needs you most."

"How can you say that? I've seen him through the worst!" Becca's temper flared now. That emotion was easy to let run free and fierce. It drove away the pain, if only for a moment. She snarled at Emily. It was so simple for Emily to judge, from the safety of her contented marriage, secure in her husband's love, but she had no idea how Becca was suffering, would suffer until she had put some distance between her and Mack.

"Did you?" Emily asked archly.

"I nursed him back from death." Becca didn't want to think about the words she had thrown at Mack, knowing she had only spared him for death of another kind.

"Did you?" Emily asked again, giving her a knowing look. "Is he whole and well?"

"I cannot heal him." Desperate to leave now, Becca wondered if she dared travel at night. She didn't want to think about that, how she had failed him. Emily was right, and yet that still changed nothing, would change nothing.

"Not if you are in Boonesborough." Emily delivered her final stinging blow and left the kitchen.

Cutter stared after her before turning back to Becca. "I cannot begin to understand what goes on in the minds of women. I do know two things. The first is that he loves you and needs you. That is why he risked his life to return to you."

"So you won't take me to Boonesborough." Becca's shoulders sagged at the very idea of making the trip on her own. She didn't care much about her own fate, but there was Caroline to consider. She could not let anything happen to her baby. She was all Becca had.

He touched her hand as he walked past her to the door. "That is the second thing. I will take you tomorrow. I don't know if it's right, but I will take you."

* * *

Emily gave her a hard hug and swiped at her eyes with her shawl. "Are you sure about this? I'm sorry for what I said last night. I just so hate to be wrong, and I was very sure you and Mack were right for each other."

"You weren't wrong; it's Mack that needs convincing." Becca gave her a tremulous smile that took more strength than she expected. "Thank you for everything you've done. You've been very kind."

"Pish, posh. Kindness is for strangers, and we are friends." Emily hugged her again. "I'm going to miss you. Are you sure you won't stay? We can always send *him* away."

Now Becca had to wipe tears away. She had never felt so cared for as she had here at Cutright's Station. She had never felt she belonged before. She had never felt loved before. And she was leaving it all behind. It was the hardest thing she had ever had to do.

"It's for the best." She mounted, and Ruth handed Caroline up to her.

"You take care of that baby," Becca said softly and squeezed the other woman's hand. "And I'll take care of mine."

"Thank you for everything, Miss Becca, for everything you done." Ruth dabbed at her eyes in unconscious imitation of her employer.

"No thanks is necessary among friends."

Knowing she couldn't stand any more good-byes, Becca kneed her horse into motion and rode out through the station gates without looking once toward the cabin where she knew Mack lay.

* * *

Mack frowned at Reuben as he set the tray down beside the bed, spilling broth and water in the process. "You're making a mess."

"I was never no house boy, and you know it, so be glad there's anything left in them things by the time I get it here." Reuben jerked the quilt off Mack and poked at the bandage on his shoulder.

Mack swatted his hand away. "Don't touch me. You probably didn't wash that hand today, and Becca says you gotta stay clean to keep infection away."

"I washed just afore I came in." Reuben reached for the bandage again. "Miss Emily tole me to."

Mack jerked out of reach and paid for the sudden movement with sharp jabs of pain in the shoulder and leg. "Clean or not, I don't want you touching me with those hams."

Reuben shrugged. "Okay, you want smaller hands, I send Tad in. His fingers aren't so big and scarred, but I bet my touch is gentler. Always worked when I was doctoring the horses."

"I'm not a horse."

"No. Yer just thickheaded enough to be a mule. No mistakin' you for a horse." Chuckling at his own joke, Reuben moved to the door.

"I don't want Tad either."

"Those yer only two choices, so choose." Reuben waited, one hand on the door latch.

"Why can't one of the women come?" Mack really wanted to know why Becca couldn't come, wouldn't

come, but he knew. Still, that didn't stop the need
to see her.

"Not a matter of can't." Reuben grinned toothily.
"Won't."

"What do you mean won't?" Mack scowled. "I'm
a sick man; don't they care if I die?"

"Not much, according to Miss Emily. She said she
cared enough not to stop us from taking care of
you, and even fixed this tray up for me, all the while
muttering about how she hoped you choked on it,
but she said she didn't want to see you and that was
that. My Ruth said some things not bear repeatin'."
Reuben shook his head.

Mack noticed there was one woman Reuben did
not mention, but he thought better of asking after
her. She would come to him. She always had.

"If that's the way it is, then you better give it a
try," Mack said grudgingly. "I've seen Tad's handiwork
before, and that boy's all thumbs. I'd just as soon he
not torture me."

Reuben changed the bandages with a minimum of
pain and discomfort. While his touch was not as gentle
as Becca's, his big hands moved with surprising grace
and tenderness. However, long after the black man
had left him alone again, Mack lay still and tried to
will the throbbing pain in his wounds to stop.

He needed to heal quickly so he could get away
from Cutright's Station and all its temptations, but
most of all, he needed to put as much distance
between him and Becca as he could.

Last night when he had seen her tears glistening
in the candlelight, he had almost broken down—

almost given in to the urge to hold her and make her promises there was no way he could keep. And that would be the very thing that destroyed her. Mack would not allow that to happen. He could not allow that to happen. The longer she stayed away from him the better.

Mack suffered the feminine wall of silence for days as he slowly healed and regained his strength. Reuben tended his wounds. Tad brought him meals. Cutter brought him news of Indian sign—of which there was none—and the Kentuckian's talk of revenge for Blue Licks—of which there was much. None of the three gave him any news of Becca.

Her name was constantly on the tip of his tongue, but he resisted the temptation to ask after her. He knew she was right to stay away, although her stubbornness surprised him. He had never thought she could stay apart from him for so long.

Each day he grew stronger and spent less time sleeping. He had even tried to hobble around the cabin a bit on his own. Although this morning when Tad had brought him his breakfast, Tad had caught Mack at it and run off quickly to tattle, Mack was sure.

He smiled smugly as he fell back onto the bed, wincing at the jarring pain that caused in his shoulder and leg. Becca would come running now. If he had remembered it would be that simple to fetch her to his side, he would have tried this trick days ago.

When the door opened moments later, it was not Becca who marched into the cabin, but Emily. "I swear, McGee, you don't have the sense God gave a squirrel. Do you want to bring that fever back?"

"What do you care?" He knew it sounded childish, but he couldn't stop the disappointment he felt that Becca still hadn't come. He had been so sure she would.

"I just hate to see all Becca's work go to waste." Setting down the tray she had carried in, she put her hands on her hips and looked him up and down.

"She doesn't seem to care overmuch about that, so why let it bother you." He scowled.

"Now, why do you say that?" Emily's tone was ominously quiet.

"She hasn't been to see me for a week, that's why!"

"Why do you care?" Emily threw his words back at him. "You were the one who sent her away, after all."

"She never paid any attention to that before, why now?"

"Maybe because she finally realized she loves you. Women don't take too kindly to having their hearts thrown back in their faces."

"She has no business loving me. Nothing can come of it."

Emily raised an eyebrow and gave him a cool, superior look. "If that is the case, then you won't care that she's gone."

"Gone? How can she be gone?" Mack stared at Emily, stunned by her news. That was the last thing he had expected. How could Becca leave him?

"Cutter took her to Boonesborough a week ago today." Emily folded her arms across her chest and gave him a chilling look. "She may well be on her way to Virginia now. That was her plan. Not much of a plan, but better than the one you've got, to my way of thinking."

"What right did Cutter have to take her to Boonesborough?" Mack asked darkly. How could she be gone? How could she leave him?

"What right?" Emily's eyes snapped sparks at him. "She asked him for help and he gave it. What right do you have to question either Cutter or Becca?"

Mack opened his mouth and then shut it again. She was right, as much as he hated to admit it. He had no rights where Becca was concerned, but that didn't stop the feeling of betrayal.

Emily smirked. "Good choice. It's the most sensible thing you've done in quite some time. Now lie still and let me check those wounds."

He lay back, still and tight-lipped, as Emily changed his bandages. When she was done she collected the old bandages, the cloths and water she had used to clean his wounds, and the empty bowl and mug from his breakfast. All in silence. He knew he was being punished, but he was damned if he was going to speak to the woman when he knew that would only invite another tongue-lashing.

After surveying him with a frosty glance, she turned away and took a step toward the door. Then she slammed the tray down on the table with a crash and turned on him.

Mack braced himself for the onslaught. He should have known escape would not be so easy, not when Emily had been saving up words for a week.

"The way I see it, Silas McGee, if the devil had wanted your rotten soul, then he would have taken it at Blue Licks, but he didn't. What does that tell you? Maybe you've been spared for a reason. Maybe that reason is Rebecca Wallace. Think on that."

He did. He had nothing else to do but think on that, so he thought for the remainder of the day and most of the night. He thought about what Emily had said to him, but mostly he thought about Becca and what she had asked of him.

When morning came and Tad brought him his breakfast, he found Mack dressed and painfully experimenting with the crutch Reuben had carved him.

"What's this?" Tad asked cautiously as he set the tray down, his gaze flickering toward the door.

"Something I should have done a long time ago." Mack sank heavily onto the table bench, nearly tilting it in the process. He gritted his teeth and fought through the wave of pain in his leg. It hurt like hell, but he could bear it. Just.

Tad edged toward the door, and Mack waved him on.

"You go ahead and tell Emily and Cutter what I'm about. I know that's what you're dying to do. Go ahead and spread your tale, then gather my long rifle and packs, and saddle Joseph."

"But . . ." Tad hesitated, his hand on the latch.

"Just do it." Mack gave him a smile and tucked into the food the boy had delivered. He would need his strength for what he had planned.

CHAPTER 24

"Is there any chance of changing your mind?" Cutter asked as he walked beside Mack, watching his every painful limp across the station yard.

"No. I should have done this long ago." Mack gritted his teeth as he reached Joseph and mounted.

Once in the saddle, he closed his eyes and let the waves of pain rise over him. When the worst was past, he grinned down into Cutter's anxious face. "Nothing to worry about."

"I didn't drag your sorry hide all the way back from Blue Licks just to watch you die from sheer foolishness." Cutter's rough tone did not quite disguise his worry.

Mack glanced at the gates, wanting to be off. He finally had a purpose, and he wanted to be about it. However, Cutter had saved his life, as had Emily in her own way. "It is your own fault; you are the one who took her to Boonesborough." He understood why Cutter had done it, but that didn't mean he had to like it. He smiled a bit to show there were no hard feelings.

"She was going to Boonesborough with or without me," Cutter answered. "Would you have me let her go off on her own?"

"I would have had her not go off at all."

"And I would have you wait another day or so," Cutter returned.

Mack grinned. "Then, we are even."

"You are becoming a mother hen in your old age, husband." Emily tucked her arm through Cutter's and smiled up at Mack. "He'll do well enough. If he sickens a little on the journey, that will be all to the better."

"You once loved me. Now you do not care about me at all." Mack gave her a mournful look, his heart lighter now that he knew he would see Becca before the day was out.

"I never loved you; you just wished it." She leaned against her husband's shoulder and rested a hand on the mound of her stomach. "I am not wishing you ill, but thought if you did not look entirely well, then Becca would show you more sympathy."

"You best practice a hangdog look during the ride." Cutter gave his wife a sidelong glance. "For we both know women have little sympathy in them unless they know they've defeated you."

Emily's scolding voice followed Mack out the station gates as he headed for Boonesborough. He smiled at the sound, his heart lighter than it had been in his memory.

He rode on, even as the afternoon sun faded behind a mist of rain that his hat and upturned collar could do nothing to dispel. Soon he was so wet and cold, he wondered if Emily had arranged this weather just so he would arrive at Boonesborough looking as dejected as she could want.

The rain followed him to the gates of the fort, where once hailed inside by the men on the wall, he found no one on the green to witness his dejection but a speckled pig lying blissfully in a wallow of mud.

However, by the time he had dismounted, clinging to Joseph as the wave of pain and weakness swept over him in repayment for the effort, a group of boys had emerged from one of the cabins to torment the pig from its wallow. They pointed him to a cabin on the far side of the green when he asked about Becca.

He stood outside the cabin door for a long moment, dripping on the step, suddenly unsure of his welcome. True, she loved him, but that did not mean she would be so quick to forgive him. His lips curved into a smile as he raised his hand to knock on the door. It might be fun to convince her to forgive him, for she would, he knew, in the end.

A pale waif of a girl answered the door, a drooling, wide-eyed baby on her hip. When he asked about Becca, she gave him a look of confusion.

"She's gone. I don't know where she went."

"Gone?" Panic struck through him. He would follow her to Virginia if necessary, but he had hoped, no, counted on her being here in Boonesborough.

"Jimmy here was up half the night." The girl joggled the baby on her hip to signal who Jimmy might be, if there was any doubt. "He's teething. I was having a nap myself, the rain was so soothing, and when I woke up she was gone."

Mack's tension eased. "So she is here, somewhere in the fort."

"Where else would she be?" The girl gave him a look of confusion.

He stepped out of the mist like a miracle. Her heart stopped for a moment, as she thought she had conjured him out of thin air. Then Mack smiled, and Becca's heart started again with a jolt.

"What brings you here?" she asked, afraid to take hope from the warmth she saw in his eyes and yet needing to.

"I discovered something very simple when I woke up and you were gone."

She tried to speak, but her mouth had gone dry. She wet her lips. "What is that?"

"That you are worth living for, Becca."

"Oh, Mack." Letting the water bucket fall from her numb fingers, splashing still more water against her sodden skirts, she touched her hand to her throat in a helpless gesture. There was a lump of words caught there. She didn't know what to say or do or think or feel. No, that was wrong; she knew what to feel. It swept through her, a buoyant feeling she scarcely recognized, for it was stronger and deeper than it had felt before.

"Is that all you can say?" His lopsided grin was almost her undoing.

Her knees went so weak she was afraid to take a step. "What do you want me to say?"

"Yes."

"Yes?" Her head was spinning. Why hadn't he touched her yet?

"Then, you will?"

"Will what?"

"Marry me, of course. Isn't that what we're talking about?"

"I don't know." The lump gone from her throat, she laughed for the sheer joy of it. "You're talking in riddles again, and I don't know anything except the fact that you haven't told me you love me yet."

"I love you, Rebecca Wallace soon-to-be McGee. Always and forever."

Then, not knowing who had taken the first step, who had touched whom first, she was in his arms. "Always and forever," she whispered against his lips.

EPILOGUE

"You can scream if that will help." Mack's eyes were filled with worry as Becca panted her way through another contraction. "Emily screamed a lot, both times."

"I was screaming at my husband, if you remember correctly." Emily gave him a look as she massaged Becca's belly. "But he is right, Becca. You can scream if you like."

Giving her husband's pale face a close study, Becca attempted a smile that turned into more of a grimace as another contraction started. "I'll manage without screaming, takes too much energy."

"I would rather suffer myself than see you suffer." Mack winced as Becca squeezed his hand through the next contraction.

As soon as Becca released her grip on Mack's hand, Ruth stepped forward. "Mr. Mack, you best see to boiling some water." She took the expectant father by the arm and guided him to the door. "We gonna need lots of water."

As the door shut behind them, Becca heard Ruth talking about the need for rabbit stew.

"This ain't no place for a man." Ruth bustled back in within a few moments. "Now you can scream without worryin' 'bout him worryin' 'bout you."

"Rabbit stew?" Emily asked pointedly.

Ruth laughed. "You'd think with them three babies and Miss Ima running about, those men wouldn't have time to worry 'bout nothing else; but they is, so I figured to give them something else to think on."

Becca laughed breathlessly. "You were right, Ruth. I was getting worried that I might have to make room to let Mack lie down beside me."

"He was looking quite pale." It was Emily's turn to wince as Becca gripped her hand. "But I would have just put him on the floor. If you'd thought of that solution nine months ago, you wouldn't be here now."

"You are talking about the father of my child." Becca panted. "The child who intends to be born right now."

Emily and Ruth moved in a frenetic dance to tend to the birth, and Becca's son was born in a slippery rush of blood and pain that culminated in a surge of triumph when she heard her child's first cry.

Emily lay the baby in Becca's arms as they delivered the afterbirth.

Becca looked into her child's tiny, red angry face and fell in love. She protested when Ruth took the child to clean him, but he was quickly returned to her arms where she opened her bodice to let him nurse.

Silence reigned in the cabin as the door flung open with a crash to admit a wild-eyed Mack.

"I've got two kettles on the fire. Will that be enough water or should—" His mouth snapped shut as he caught sight of the baby.

Becca smiled at his look of confusion. "Come meet your son."

The two other women moved out the door, calling Caroline to come meet her brother, but Becca's focus shrank to the sense of wonder she saw on her husband's face.

Mack first caressed Becca's cheek and then reached a hesitant hand toward his son. When he touched one tiny fist with a finger, the newest McGee seized it in a tight grip.

The new father broke into a grin. "He's a strong little man."

"Just like his father." Her heart was so full, Becca thought she could never be happier.

"No, like his mother." Mack touched her lips to stifle her protest. "Like his parents, he has a determination to meet life on his terms and a will to live to match."

Becca smiled her approval.

Deanna Mascle loves to hear from her readers. You can write to her at:

Deanna Mascle
P.O. Box 839
Winchester, KY 40392-0839

Or visit her Web site:

http://deannamascle.com.

Send a self-addressed, stamped envelope, and she will send you a signed bookplate and her personally designed bookmarks.

Merlin's Legacy

A Series From
Quinn Taylor Evans